From "White Bed", her first published story, which appeared in a feminist horror anthology in 1993, Kaaron Warren has produced powerful, disturbing fiction.

With four novels and six short story collections in print, and close to two hundred short fiction sales, Warren's award-winning fiction tackles the themes of obsession, murder, grief, despair, revenge, manipulation, death and sex.

Kaaron has won many awards such as the Shirley Jackson, Aurealis, Ditmar, Australian Shadows and ACT Writers and Publishers Awards for her novels and short fiction, including *Slights*, *The Grinding House*, *Through Splintered Walls, The Grief Hole,* and the novella "Sky". She's lived in Melbourne, Sydney and Fiji and now in Canberra with her family.

IFWG Titles by Kaaron Warren

The Grief Hole (illustrations by Keely Van Order) 2016
The Gate Theory (short story collection) 2017

PRAISE FOR KAARON'S WORK

"'The Gate Theory' is a perfect example of Kaaron Warren's accomplishment in converting different themes and subjects into dense and powerful fiction. Her stories have the tendency to insidiously crawl under the reader's skin, slithering unnoticed until they find a place from where one is unable to shake them loose after reading."
~ Dark Wolf's Fantasy Reviews

"Kaaron Warren is without doubt one of the world's leading writers of dark fiction, and *The Gate Theory* showcases her talent perfectly… Her prose is powerful, her sense of place is evocative and her imagination knows no bounds. This is the kind of book that you will remember long after you finish reading the last story."
~ M R Cosby, Stranger Designs

"Each of these stories stretches the boundaries of both storytelling and character. Warren's is a unique voice in horror. She has an ability to take us to places so utterly disturbing yet simultaneously so mundane and believable, that you start to look at people you meet with a sidelong glance. I call it The Warren Perception. It's unavoidable. Read her work and you will start to look at people as she does. This is not necessarily a good thing, but it's fascinating."
~ Alan Baxter, Thirteen O'Clock

"*Gaze Dogs*, like the other stories in this fine collection, captures the elusive quality of a dream: the strong, darkly surreal images, but also the resonant feeling. So often—in stories, as in dreams—the feeling dies away and only the image remains, a husk that has lost reference

to its once-valuable contents. The power of Warren’s stories is to hold onto both simultaneously, giving us the image–feeling complex in all its potency, and nightmares all the more frightening for being only half glimpsed.”
~ J. Ashley Smith, Spook Tapes

“All of the stories are beautifully written and subtle in the real horror they depict. Kaaron Warren’s style is dynamic and thought-provoking—it is the epitome of quiet horror. If you like your horror with an understated quality, then THE GATE THEORY is for you.”
~ Colleen Wanglund, The Horror Fiction Review

“The only warning I'm going to issue is if you read *The Gate Theory* you are going to be hooked on Ms Warren's writing style and want to read everything she has ever written…”
~ Scaryminds

The Gate Theory

Kaaron Warren

The Gate Theory

ISBN-13: 978-1-925759-54-9

V1.0
First Published in 2015

IFWG Publishing International
Melbourne, Australia
ifwgpublishing.com

Table of Contents

PURITY

Therese was clean on the inside, but her mud-slapped, filthy, stinking home—with its stacks of newspapers going back as far as she was born, spoons bent and burnt, food grown hard and crusty—kept her skin dirty. The floor all shit and mud and dropped rags.

Her mother was blind to it all, only seeing the bottle, and if Therese was living a cliché, she didn't notice. Her mother ate nothing but potato chips. She liked the ones with chicken flavour, so that's what she stank of. Not of chicken but of that yellow, chemical, thirsty smell of artificial chicken.

She knew her mother loved her. Hadn't she dumped Therese but changed her mind? Baby Therese was found abandoned at the hospital, covered with dirt, a thick, sludgy layer of it. They'd never seen a young baby so filthy. A nurse scraped it off, put it into a blood vial. Therese still has this vial of dirt. The nurse wrote, 'Dirt from Baby Therese'. The handwriting was neat, the 'i' dotted with a flower.

Her mother came to get her a week later when the love affair failed. The nurse gave her the vial of dirt, saying, "You need to keep your baby clean." Therese's mother puts on a voice when she tells this story, a low, scratchy voice, making the woman sound evil. Therese wondered how many children that nurse had and what her house looked like.

This was the last boyfriend her mother ever had. It was food she loved from then on. Food she'd eat without touching, tipping it into her mouth straight from the packet.

Therese never found out what happened to her mother to make

her want to be fat and why she was always filthy.

"I don't want you to know," her mother would say, though not knowing was worse, especially as Therese got older and realised some of the crap that could happen.

She was loved, though. She knew she was loved, and she was never hurt, always fed. Her mother was fine but dirty.

She did her homework at school because if she did it at home, greasy fingerprints would appear, a dark smear, a drop of something viscous. Her desk was neat, clean, her handwriting perfect, her work pristine.

She wasn't good at schoolwork but she persisted. Wanted to be the first in her family to finish high school and she would do it, next year. She wasn't smart with the school stuff. She worked hard at it but the letters mixed themselves up in her head and the teachers dismissed her because of how she looked. She didn't blame them for this; there were too many children. Too many problems. They'd dealt with her older brother and knew what a hopeless case he was, and they didn't even know how he lived now. Down there in the basement, pale from the lack of sun, and he blinked when he came up to the kitchen, blinked and snuffled at the garbage until she wanted to push him back down the stairs.

There were layers of shit down there. He didn't care. He was strong and when he was clean he was good-looking. He could be funny when he wanted to; the funniest person Therese knew. She copied his style, when she made people laugh. Took his wink, his timing, took the way he flapped his hands, held his head when he was telling a joke.

The joke was him, though. That was the stuff which made people laugh. Laughing at where she came from before they did gave her the power of it.

She knew she would escape. Get where it's clean.

"There's nowhere cleaner," her mother told her. "The world is a filthy place." She said this as she ate her chips. Sometimes she ate them sitting on the toilet.

Therese worked at the supermarket after school and on the weekends, saving her money.

Most people were clean there but one young customer, he came in every week, she could smell the soap on him from three registers away. He was lovely. He started to come through her register every time and they talked. Up close the soap smell was good and his fingernails were white with cleanliness. He was a laugher. After every sentence, funny or not. Sometimes he brought his grandfather, a nice, white-haired old man, bent at the shoulders, clean, neat. Therese wondered what it would be like to have a neat old man like that in your life.

One Thursday afternoon, they came through her register with grapes, cherries, lychees and apricots. The old man was dressed neatly in beige pants and a collared T-shirt, the uniform of the old man everywhere. He wore a white baseball cap with a logo of the local bowling club.

"That's a lot of fruit," she said.

"Purification," the old man said. "Nothing like fruit for purification. Skin keeps it clean inside, and you know if it's rotting because it'll be soft and bruised. You can tell if it's no good to eat. And even so, when it does rot, it leaves behind pure seed."

He and the boy laughed. Therese smiled and laughed, too, although there was nothing funny. The old man laughed harder, threw his head back, roared with it until his eyes watered. The boy gently placed his hand on the man's shoulder, calming him. The old man bent to pick up the next bag of fruit from the trolley and she saw that at the back of his cap, at the buckle, there was a red, creeping stain. It looked like blood but it could have been rust. It looked like he was leaking fluid from a small hole in his skull. She saw it everywhere, all over the shop; seeping wounds, pus, fat rotten flesh pushing at skin to get out. The boy slipped a packet of gum into his pocket; the old man stole a chocolate bar.

He stood and caught her staring. Smiled. "These things happen slowly," he said. "Impurities begin to leak out. Better out than in, I say." He and the boy laughed again, so loudly people turned to look, but she didn't care. She wanted to laugh with them, laugh like that.

Therese's mother laughed a lot. Mid-sentence, she'd chuckle. If the milk was sour, she'd laugh. If kids threw eggs at the house, she'd laugh. When Therese was fourteen, her first period came, messy and painful. Her mother laughed. "It happens to all of us," she said, and directed Therese to scrabble in this cupboard and that, looking for sanitary napkins. She found a sticky, dusty packet behind some rusty tins of peas and she had to use them until she got to a shop.

"I stopped long ago, darling, when they took my insides out. You know what you did to my insides, don't you? Tore them up like a tiny Jack the Ripper." Her mother laughed at this.

There are times when the whole family fell into fits of hysterical laughter. Sugar-high laughter. This was when her aunties came over with cakes and lollies, lemonade, "Gotta feed you up", no intention of teaching good eating habits because as long as their sister was fat and dirty, they were better. Other times, the neighbourhood mothers took pity on her and invited her over for meals. They'd trick out ways to get her clean, they'd give her their kids' clothes and she loved the smell of them, the soap she could smell in there, the starch from the iron.

The old man and his grandson paid for their fruit.

"You should join us, Therese," the old man said. "Come and share the fruit with us." He trembled and she wondered if he was nervous.

His grandson nodded. "There'll be lots of people there tonight. We have a lot of friends."

Therese looked around, not sure if they were talking to her.

The old man wrote down the address on the back of his receipt. "You'll have a laugh, Therese. Life is always better with laughter."

She stopped at a clothing shop on the way home, wanting brand-new things which hadn't been touched by her mother, by her house. She chose badly, though, and regretted it once she'd showered and dressed. A pink, fluffy skirt and a tight shiny red singlet top. Brand-new, unwashed, as clean as she could want. But it all itched and the skirt was too short.

She caught two buses to a large house in the suburbs. Three storeys, it seemed to extend out the back a long way. There were lights all around it and the lawns were lush and neat.

The grandson was waiting on the front door step. His name was Daniel. "We're always adding to it," he said. "I think the original house was a tin shack."

"Bit like my mother," she said, getting in early with the jokes. "She's been expanding since she was fifteen."

He laughed, really laughed, and she was glad he got her humour.

Inside, the place was surprisingly coherent. The entrance had three or four doors off it and a large staircase rising upstairs. Four people chattered against the walls, one nibbling a crumbly pastry, making Therese feel suddenly hungry.

"Through here. We're just in time to hear him speak."

"Who?" They hadn't warned her about any speaker. Therese pushed open the heavy door and stepped inside. It was the size of a small hall and full of people. It was cold; goosebumps formed and she felt her hair prickle.

She bent to scrabble a jumper from her backpack but a hand on her shoulder stopped her.

Daniel said. "Cold is purifying."

The gaps around them filled and she couldn't move. Standing room only.

On a tall stool at the front of the room sat the grandfather. He looked different; bigger, broader. Silvery grey hair, face barely lined, clear blue eyes.

"I am Calum," he said. He smiled, broad white teeth slightly sharp. "I am the Jester. I sit before you a humble man." There was laughter. A chuckle or two. Therese was surprised but waited for more before reacting. She shivered; it was freezing in the room. Around her, others shivered, too. Even the mass of bodies didn't help, though she thought it would eventually.

He spoke on. Nonsense in a deep voice. About football and fame and pressure and what he had for lunch. Music played beneath his voice and that explained why people swayed, butt cheek to butt cheek.

They laughed. It began quietly, but when he started talking about his pyjamas, they were hysterical. They wept, they sweated, clear fluids leaking.

Therese felt embarrassed for them. A woman three rows down wet her pants and no one seemed to notice. They laughed as if they'd forgotten how and were copying what they'd seen on television. Wide mouths, noise pouring out with no mirth in it.

Someone heehawed like a donkey.

She watched them. The dirtiness of their sweat. It came out clean, but dust, there was always dust, clung to them, muddying their skin. She squeezed her eyes tight.

"Don't worry," Daniel whispered. "They'll wash and be clean for the afternoon meal."

At the thought of food, her stomach growled.

"Lunch?"

"We don't have the standard three meals. We have breakfast at dawn and then one meal between when you would normally have lunch and dinner. He says it's better to go to sleep with digested food in your stomach."

"That makes sense, it really does," Therese said. She hated the late-night, thrown-together meals at home. Leftovers of a week ago tossed with cheese, covered with melted butter and crushed potato chips and baked, all bad news and toilet stink.

She felt a hand poke in her ribs and turned, holding her side.

A middle-aged man glared at her. His face was runnelled with tear tracks; was he the donkey laugher?

"How dare you not laugh? Who do you think you are?"

"You're not laughing right now," she said.

He poked her again with his long, hairy forefinger, opened his mouth and brayed.

The woman next to her pinched her. "If you don't laugh, you don't belong."

Daniel poked her too, but sexy, sexy. He moved up the front, tugging her hand to take her with him and soon he was rolling in the aisle, hysterical.

Calum spoke, his voice loud over the laughter, but no one cared what he said. Therese listened as he talked about his childhood.

"Shivering is another hysteria," he said. "One year, when I was at high school, there was a heat wave. We stood in the courtyard, lined up, listening to speeches. We were not being respectful, we did not listen, we would fail and we would all have to work in petrol stations for life, be fat, pimply, greasy adults. We were too hot to listen.

"It was so hot the children were panting, and one girl fainted, then another. I looked at this and I felt something sharp, I smelled orange peel, but I didn't faint. I began to shiver uncontrollably.

"A friend touched me and he began to shiver as well, calling to his girlfriend, 'Cold! It's cold!' and there was no sense to it but soon every child was fainted or shivering and the principal lost his job over it and ended up tutoring maths to bored children. He no longer had parents sucking up to him, wanting favours. He had people crossing the street to avoid him.

"I did my final-year assignment on the hysteria. I took the girl who'd first fainted out a few times, seeing if there was something in both of us which made it happen. She looked close to fainting most of the time. I wondered if it was a scent, something to set people off. Was that it?

"I tried to make her faint, just by talking to her. But it made her so nervous that she giggled and couldn't stop. She couldn't even eat her chocolate mousse, kept spluttering it out. The waiter started laughing, and others. I watched it move like a wave.

"I spent years trying to find the source. The cause of it. But there is none. Not even love of God."

Therese walked close to him, until she stood at his feet, staring at him. Listening.

"Are you ready to laugh?" he said.

She nodded.

He opened his mouth so wide she could see down his throat, and he began to laugh. He took her face in his hands, made her look him in the eyes, and he laughed until she started and she knew this was it; she would not be able to stop.

A chuckle at first; sardonic, she thought, a sardonic chuckle. She thought she'd fake it but she didn't have to. It was like she'd lost control of her body; she shivered, her limbs weak, her gut filled with butterflies and she laughed so hard her muscles ached.

She took to laughing at a speed which was frightening. And she laughed so hard old wounds opened, and she bled, her arms, her legs, slick with blood: she made patterns on the lino with it, dark red finger painting. Therese laughed so hard a blood vessel popped in her eyes. And that became the goal. Even the Jester took to it, bleeding quietly. He'd score his thighs with a sharp knife and the others did it, too.

Therese tried to watch it dispassionately, tried to understand it, and looked for physical causes for the hysteria; incense, heavy breathing, drugs, alcohol, hypnosis. She saw none of this.

She saw things she didn't believe possible. She saw people collapse, not breathing, then wake with their fillings turned to gold. She saw this; mouths full of gold.

"People will do anything for money," Calum said as the numbers grew, as word got out. Only Therese listened to the words; the others laughed.

"Laugh until you sweat. Until you bleed. That is how you are purified." Daniel rolled at Calum's feet and he did bleed, from the eyes and the ears. Therese bent and gently wiped the blood away.

After each session, sometimes days-long, a cleaning crew would go through. Therese loved the meeting hall after this cleaning. Her eyes would sting from the bleach, but the smell and the shine were all she'd ever wanted.

Calum did not remind her of her grandfather, although they were of an age.

Her grandfather had walked the streets in rags held together by bodily secretions. They drove past him every day on the school bus. He knew she was aboard, would raise his hand in greeting. His teeth were rotted in his head, his gums swollen, and he no longer called out loud.

That was where she came from, that empty poverty. He was jailed thirty-five years for spitting at a cop, because he had HIV AIDS.

Calum trembled and sat stiffly. Only Therese noticed this.

"Are you all right, Jester?" she said.

"I embrace the symptoms. They will make me pure." But his stiffness and tremors lasted into meals, in the evenings, in quiet times when there was no laughter.

Therese went to a doctor and, while she was being examined, asked about her 'grandfather' and his tremors.

"It sounds like it could be Parkinson's. You need to get him to come in for tests. There are drugs to control it. We need to be careful, though. Some of the drugs can lead to compulsive, self-rewarding behaviour. Gambling, sex, shopping."

"Laughter?" she asked.

"Yeah, I'd say. Laughter releases the pleasure chemical, too."

Calum did not deny it. "It's my family's impure blood."

"And you use your drug on the people?"

"Sometimes, to help things along. Not always, though. It's themselves."

Those who laughed themselves close to death awakened with no memory. Every moment was their first.

Calum said, "This is a good thing. Clearing your mind of the past, cleaning out bad memories, will make you happy. We are safe here from the cruelties of the world."

They laughed. Therese watched the clear fluids leaking from them. When people first arrived they leaked cloudy stuff, muddy stuff, but soon the liquids flowed clear, like from a well-done roast chicken.

The Jester sat in a large armchair. He was a big man but he looked small in its cushions.

"You seem happy, Therese."

Fresh from the shower, her skin still felt clean. Her clothes clean. It would be an hour or more before the dirt started to cling.

She turned around for him, her arms spread wide. "Do you like me happy?"

He smiled. "Clean and happy, you are at your most beautiful."

He leapt about like a jester, jumping foolishly to make people laugh.

"I come from a long line of jesters. Not all of them funny like me. One dear man so upset his crowd they kicked him down the stairs. Broke his neck as if he were a chicken. My mum used to say I had the spirit of him in me. His essence."

The audience laughed, laughed louder.

"She said that as the jester died, he laughed once, a bitter choke full of hate and regret. The basement servant stood by, and he had a small pot he'd emptied of beer that very moment. He captured that laugh which came out brown and oozy. Kept it for good, a time of need. But while there were many times of need, there never was one strong enough for the essence. This is how time passes. We wait and wait for a moment that never comes. We should make the moment, take it. That's what we should do."

The infection was full in them now, and they were out of their seats, roaring with laughter. Children, too, filled with pure hysteria.

"My mother came into the essence when she was born. Her father told her, save it for the end of the world.

"But along the way I was born. Born sad, I was, full of misery and despair. Do you see?"

They saw, a hundred of them screaming his name.

"I didn't feel right in the world. It seemed so dirty and cruel. So I tried to take myself out of it."

Screams of laughter, louder from those who'd tried themselves.

"My mother found me with the gun all ready. I wanted to be sure. She told me to wait, she was very calm, and she brought me the essence of that old jester. It was a bitter liquid, thick like cough syrup, but it filled me with a good humour which has not left me yet. Who else puts any faith in purity? Who else cares? Drinkers like their vodka pure. Holistic people like their food pure. Is food ever pure? There is damage along the way, I think." This is what he told them. "Truth is confession. You must tell me all."

And they did. All their secrets.

"Pain is truth, beauty and purity. Scars are pain and they tell the story of an impure life. Beauty is without scarring. Do you understand that you are not beautiful? You think you are but not at all."

They gave him their bank details because he said that only truth, beauty and purity will give them wealth. They had mouths full of gold fillings and they had no memory.

"You are not alone, or special. Once you're gone it's like you were never there. All you can do is lead a pure life, worship the life you are given."

"I was threatened with a year of ugliness if I didn't pass on a breast cancer chain letter," Therese said.

He laughed. "All your ugliness is on your skin and your own actions didn't cause that. There is clear blood running in your veins, because to purify something you need to corrupt it first. Fruit rots, leaving behind a beautiful seed. Remember?" It seemed so long ago, that time in the supermarket. A lifetime ago.

She still worked there, though she brought the groceries to the Jester now. He no longer needed to shop. Sometimes Daniel would meet her, help her take the things home, and she liked those times.

They would drive in the car, the groceries rattling in the back seat, and it was normal. Average. The sort of thing people did.

Then he would laugh, and she would, and they were back in that again. Daniel always slipped something into his pocket; homage to the Jester. Therese would smile, look away. It didn't bother her.

Until the day he was caught.

He'd taken a pen, a good heavy one for the Jester. Therese didn't see him do it, which should have helped when she was questioned later, but didn't.

He was caught as they walked out the door. The fact he laughed at them…no security man likes being laughed at. They wouldn't be in the job if they could deal with people laughing at them. So he was taken to the police station. He said to Therese, "Don't let them laugh without me. Okay? Don't let him lead a meeting."

The Jester was furious. "How dare they take our people? How is he to laugh in there? We must laugh as we have never laughed before." He was quiet for a moment. "Therese, this town is so dirty. So full of pus it's coming through the seams."

This seemed an exaggeration to her, and she wondered if perhaps the scales were lifting from her eyes.

"Daniel will be home soon. They'll only keep him a couple of hours. He said we should wait for him. That we should not have a meeting without him."

"This town is filthy, Therese. We must laugh, laugh. This is for Daniel's sake, Therese."

"We can't have a meeting without him."

"We can, you know."

That afternoon, as the meeting began, he said, "We have no control over how it will affect people. That is not our business. Our business is purity, our business is to take what has been cleansed and work with it. You must break something down before you can cleanse it. At least this way there is only one emotion out of control.

Can you imagine Hatred? Or Lust? Or Anger? These things will cause damage to all around them. I have never done anything wrong. Even as a child my inner voice was very loud.

"Laugh, my friends, laugh as you have never laughed before. Let them hear your spirit, let them join us." Pachelbel's Canon played, soft, gentle, rhythmic.

People began to laugh. Laughed so hard their eyeballs were bloody, their bones cracked, and they couldn't breathe.

"Laugh to purify this city, laugh for Daniel, laugh as if you have nothing to live for."

Laughter became pain. Therese's guts were dagger-struck, her bones mallet-shattered, her tongue split in two, her teeth cracked, her eyes swelled out of her head, but she could not stop. She felt her breath leaving, the oxygen out of her body, as blackness filled her eyes and she knew nothing more.

Hot dragon's breath on her face. She opened her eyes. Daniel bent over her, smiling.

"Welcome back from the dead, Therese."

She sat up. Around her, bodies lay; bloodied, emptied, pure. She pulled herself tall and didn't scream, though she took Daniel's hand. She turned her head, looking for the Jester.

"I'm here, Therese." He sat on his stool. He looked exhausted, almost bored.

"Did you die also?"

"Not this time." He slid off the stool, leaning heavily on Daniel's shoulder.

Daniel helped them both limp forward. His face was drawn, tears on his cheeks. "I told you not to run the meeting." He wept as they picked their way through the dead. Sirens in the distance.

"It's so terrible."

"It is. He can't control them like I do. But it is good. We have purified them all. Pain, beauty, purity. They are happy. It's all over."

She bent down to look at a beautiful eagle necklace around the neck of a young girl.

"Take it," he said, spittle-voiced. "Take whatever you want. But we'll need to hurry."

They picked like vultures off the laughing dead; money, jewellery, iPods, phones; picked and stashed the goods into four green shopping bags.

"How do you feel?" Daniel said once they were out of the house and travelling in their air-conditioned, perfumed sedan.

"I feel dirty on the surface but within I feel cleansed."

"Pure?"

"Pure."

She had a gash on her forehead from falling.

"That will heal to a beautiful scar," he said. "What does it feel like to think you are dead? To wake up among the dead?"

"I can see more sharply. Edges are clearer. I see bruises I couldn't see before."

"That's emotional bruising. What you see is heartbreak, or guilt, or fear."

"It really was like sleep. But it was much darker. Blanker. And re-birthing was like waking from a sleep supposed to last five days but you wake up after two."

The Jester shook. He tried to sip a soft drink, chinotto, bitter, but he could not lift it to his mouth.

He took Therese's hand. "My dear daughter."

The comfort those words gave her were beyond anything she had known. Her own father said fuck, fuck off, fuck you, and she'd watch him bleed to death in a pub brawl. Hiding under the table with her Barbie dolls.

"I think another town beckons," Daniel said.

She was quiet.

"A problem?"

"My mother. I hate to leave her alone in her filth. And my brother."

"We can bring them or we can purify them where they sit."

Could she do it? Burn the filthy house down, burn the clothes, the papers, the rotting carpet, the decades of boxes? The chocolate wrappers?

Daniel said, "It's up to you to decide. Then we'll spend some money. We'll hire a cleaner to scrub as we walk, scrabble on the ground before us to make sure we step clean. We'll buy a comedy club for you to star in."

Therese smiled. She still hadn't figured out what it was she would have to do for him to thank him for giving her her life back. She saw through the Jester at least; overblown, arrogant man. He was kind, though, and she admired that. And the way he could draw an audience, that was something she wanted to learn. She would walk on with him, bringing people to laughter.

At the side of the road there were dead cows, burnt, hit by lightning perhaps, direct hit. Therese thought, We are like a bushfire, coming suddenly and burning a place to the ground. Bushfires clear the land to make it ready for new growth. That is what we are doing.

There was a smell in the air, a sweet smell, which made them smile. Each smelled something different.

In the back seat, her mother hummed softly. They'd paid a nurse to clean her up and now, covered with perfume and creams, her white hair soft around her face, Therese felt like hugging her. Her brother had refused to leave, although the Jester had made him laugh.

"Better out than in," Calum said, and they drove on to select the next town to be gifted with purity.

That Girl

St Martin's was clean, you could say that at least. Apart from the fine mist of leg hair, that is. I watched as Sangeeta ("You know me. I am Sangeeta.") crawled through the women's legs, a long piece of thread hanging from between her teeth. She stroked a shin, a knee, looking for hairs to pluck.

"Come on, Sangeeta. All the ladies are bald, now. You'll have to find a dog." The head nurse was very kind when there were visitors, the inmates told me.

They sat along the wide verandah that wrapped around their dorm. Like many verandahs in Fiji, it acted as their social centre. It was the only place in the hospital with comfortable chairs. The dining hall, in a collapsing once-white building behind the dorm, had hard chairs designed to make you eat quickly: the art therapy room, across the loosely-pebbled driveway, had stools. This was one of the things I wanted to change; put comfy chairs in so the women could sit and stitch, or paint, or weave. At present they made small pandanus fans and carved turtles from soap, to be sold at the annual bazaar. My funding covered a month, and came from a wealthy Australian woman who'd visited St Martin's and been depressed at the state of the art therapy room, with paintings so old there was more dust than paint. They had no supplies at all. My benefactor hired me to sort out the physical therapy room, perhaps train the nurses in some art techniques. The nurses loved the sessions with me and used them to gossip, mostly.

Sangeeta dragged herself up using the band of my skirt. "You've got too many hairs in your eyebrows. And your lip is like a hairy worm."

I turned a stare on her and she shrank.

The head-nurse said, "You comment on our guest's appearance? Are you perfect? There are things you will need to learn, Sangeeta. If you want to return to your life in Suva."

Sangeeta primped her hair. "I am a beauty therapist. Of course I am beautiful." Her face was deeply scarred by acne. Open wounds went septic so easily in the tropics. There was a red slash across her throat, vivid shiny skin, and two of her fingers were bent sideways. The fingernails were painted and chipped, bitten to the quick. "I studied in Australia. I married an Australian man but he went mad every full moon."

"Of course he did," the head nurse said. "He was cursed on your honeymoon at Raki Raki."

"He upset the witches. He didn't believe they were witches and took a photo of me kissing one of their pigs. Then he said I smelled like bacon and could not make love to me."

"You are blessed," one of the other inmates said. "You will die untouched."

"My second husband turned out to be gay," Sangeeta said, all the time the thread hanging from her mouth. She held the thread taut. "Can I pluck your hairs? Make you smooth?"

The other women set up a clamor, all wanting to do something for me. To me.

Only the old lady at the end of the verandah sat quietly, her lips moving. I walked over to her and bent my head down. "What is it, dear?" I said.

"I am that girl," she said. "I am that girl."

She was very thin. Her skin was wrinkled, looking like folds of brown velvet—a hand-made soft toy for an ungrateful child.

"I am that girl," the old woman said. Not much else. She would demand more porridge if it were on, and sometimes sing if the prayer was in Hindi. I would learn all this in the next few days.

She grabbed at me with sharp fingernails. They should have been clean; everything else was here, but I saw a dark red ridge I didn't like. If she was a painter I would have guessed at Russet Red, but she was not a painter. A strong smell of bleach filled the air. I suspected it was their only cleaning fluid.

"What girl does she mean?"

The head nurse shook her head. "We don't know. Malvika has been saying that for a long time now. She's been here since she was a teenager. Appeared one night, they say. Filthy, torn up, you've never seen such a thing, the old nurse told me. Nobody wanted her. Her family said no thank you. She's not our worst, though." She put her hand on a mess of a girl curled in a chair. "This one here came out of the womb this way. Her family kept her in a small bure at the back of their house until she got pregnant. No one knows who the father was but they say it was a dog." The poor girl looked like she'd been grown in a jar. She was twisted and folded over herself and she chewed her lip as if it were food. My fingers itched to draw her, and the old woman, too. Not as part of my funding, but for pleasure. I paint the daily details of life, to make sense of the world and here the details were vast and many layered.

After the shift was over, the head nurse took me to the suburb of Lami, where we looked at second-hand clothes which smelled so full of mould and mothballs you could never wash it out. We went into the dark, rotting shed which passed for a market. Piles of vegetable waste sat in their own sludge, but on the tables were beautiful purple eggplants, hands of bananas, small, aromatic tomatoes. The nurse talked in Fijian to the stall holders and they smiled at me, nodding, welcoming.

"Artist!" one of them said. "Oh, mangosa!"

"Mangosa means smart," the head nurse said. "She says you are smart if you are an artist. There's the dog," she whispered. She pointed at an enormous yellow mongrel. He sat with his back against a post, his back legs stretched out, his front paws lolling. He sat like a man. I've never seen balls the size of those he displayed, bigger than cricket balls and a dark grayish pink.

"He's the one they say got poor Dog Girl pregnant. They say her children are running for local council." At last she laughed and it finally sank it she was joking. I felt thick, slow and patronising, that I would believe such a thing.

I paid for the vegetables and I paid for the taxi to drop her home and take me to my flat. Local wages are so low, my per diem from my Australian benefactor was higher than her weekly wage.

We passed St Martin's on the way. "They are mental in there," the taxi driver said, tapping his forehead. When I didn't respond he twisted to look at me, the steering wheel turning with him so we veered across into traffic coming the other way. "Mental crazy," he said. "Don't go in there."

He seemed chatty, so I asked him who he thought 'that girl' might be. He looked at me in the mirror.

"It might mean anything to anyone."

"But what does it mean to you?"

"The same as it means to any taxi driver," he said. "In the story she never gets old. Fresh-faced, sparkle-eyed, she smells of mangoes in season. Not the skin part, the flesh, chopped up and sweet on the plate. She picks up a taxi near the handicraft market in town. It's always at 5:37. A lot of us won't pick up a girl from there, then. She climbs into the backseat and gives you such a smile you feel you heart melt, all thought of your family gone."

"Have you seen her?"

"No, but my brother has. She asks to go to the cemetery and if you pry and ask who is there, she will say, 'My mother.' You want to take her home and feed her. You keep driving and you can't help looking at her in the mirror because she is so beautiful. She wears no jewelry apart from a small pendant around her neck. It nestles just here." He touched his breastbone with a forefinger, then spread his fingers as if holding a breast.

"I think that's enough," I said.

"The pendant has a picture of Krisna, fat baby eating butter. You turn the corner to reach the graveyard and you wait for her to tell you where to pull in. You feel a great coldness but the door is closed. You turn around and she is gone. Nothing of her remains."

I shivered. It was an old story, true. But it frightened me.

Taxi drivers love to tell stories of the things they've seen, the people they've picked up. I dismissed it as an urban myth, but I heard it again, and again. Always a brother, or a best friend, and they always told it with a shiver, as if it hurt to talk.

On my next visit to St Martin's I walked up to the old lady, Malvika. "I am that girl," she said. Between her breasts I saw a pendant, Krisna eating butter.

"You had a taxi ride?" I asked. "Is that right?"

"I…" She nodded.

"Will you walk with me? Let's walk. I have sweets." I whispered this last to her, not wanting the others to follow. All the women here walked slowly, their feet dragging on the floor, as if their feet were lead and they were too tired, too weak, to lift them each step. The women looked up at visitors but their eagerness was frightening. They wanted to tell you, give you their stories, and they wanted treats. Sweets to suck is mostly what they craved, sugar being the easiest addiction. Sugar ran out here because the women spooned it into their pockets, poked a wet finger in there during prayer or while they swept, then sucked that sugar off.

We walked across the driveway and around behind the art therapy room. I didn't want to sit inside on the hard stools. It was dusty and stank of bananas and sweat. I wasn't sure how I'd fix it, but fix it I would have to. We found an old bench in the shade behind the building and sat down. "I told this many times," Malvika said. "A hundred. Two hundred. They stopped writing it down."

"I can write it down," I said. I took out my sketchbook and I didn't write; I drew.

"My mother died and father was happy to find a girlfriend the next day. He didn't visit my mother's grave but at least he gave me money for a taxi. I finished my job at 5:30 and went to see Mother before going home. There were not many taxis because everybody had finished work but this one stopped. This one." She closed her eyes. I thought of the head nurse's description of Malvika's arrival and my heart started to beat. I didn't need to hear this story; I would do nothing about it. But I wanted to hear it. I did . I wanted to hear of suffering and pain. I wanted to draw it on my paper, capture the detail of it.

"Tell me," I said.

"He was a nice man and asked me questions about work and school. Then he asked about boys and my body, words I didn't like. I was not brave enough to tell him to stop but I didn't answer him.

"When we reached the cemetery he pulled right inside. It was raining and he said he didn't want me to get wet though of course I would, standing out there. He stopped the car and jumped out while I gathered my things. He opened the door for me and I thought that was kind. But he didn't let me out. No."

She squeezed her hands together. "He pushed into the back seat and he took what my husband should have had. He hit me many times. As he climbed out, I tried to get out the other door but he slammed my fingers. He dragged me out into the mud and forced my face down into it. Then he did more terrible things, tearing and hurting me."

She thrust her fingers into her pocket and brought them out covered with sugar. She sucked them.

"He picked me up and shoved me into the taxi. He could have left me there but he thought of a way to cover up his crime. He drove me up the hill to the hospital and dumped me here. I couldn't speak sense for two days and by then it was too late."

"And he invented the ghost story to explain where you had gone, in case people saw you getting in his taxi?"

The old lady looked at me and smiled. "I am that girl."

I thought, You cling to your youth. You dream of being young again, before this happened to you.

The head nurse came around the corner. "There you are! You shouldn't take her away. She is very unwell. Very fragile."

I went home to paint in the afternoon light. Rain obliterated Suva Bay and was headed our way, so I had to work fast. My painting of Malvika disturbed me, because I had the sense of her as a young girl more strongly than of her as an old woman.

The hair on her chin. I knew there was a long, dark hair, but did it curl? Which side of her face was it on?

I hailed a taxi and had him stop at a roadside market, where I bought bananas and pawpaw with the change in my purse. Nobody would question me if I came with fruit.

Out of habit I asked the driver about That Girl. This one said, "She disappears. I can show you the place."

I went to Malvika although it was close to dinnertime and the hospital didn't like a break in the routine. She sat outside the door of the dorm. The other inmates used the door at the end of the verandah.

She sat bolt upright, her eyes wide open. She didn't blink. Her mouth was open and saliva had dried around her lips.

"Omigod," I said. "She's dead."

The nurse stopped me. "No, she's in a state."

The old lady's eyes were reddened and dry. I stared into them, looking for a sign of life, but nothing. There was no pulse. No breath. I remembered nothing of my first aid training and didn't want to put my mouth on her anyway.

"We must lay her flat," I said. I could do that much. The others watched me.

"You should leave her comfortable," Sangeeta said, shaking her head. She smelled of burnt hair.

"We must call the doctor," I said, but even as I spoke I was thinking, "Prussian Blue. If I mix Prussian Blue with Titanium White, water it down, I'll get her dead eyes. I'll paint an image of herself as a young girl in there, then wipe it away and paint the blank."

"She's empty," the nurse whispered to me. "Her ghost is taking a holiday. She will be back. Just wait."

Five minutes passed and I knew I had to take charge. I called for the doctor on my cell phone. He said, "No hurry. The nurses will call for the morgue when they are ready."

I squatted beside Malvika. I wouldn't get this chance again. The hair on her chin; it didn't curl.

And it happened. After ten minutes, maybe fifteen, Malvika began to twitch, blink her eyes, then she curled over into a ball and rocked.

"She…has a doctor examined her?"

"They are not interested."

"How often does this happen?"

"Sometimes. It rests her. She is happier for days afterwards."

No one else seemed concerned and I wondered if it was my western woman ways which made me so terrified of an old woman who could die and come back to life as if she was merely sleeping.

I sat quietly and sketched their night time routine. That calmed me. Malvika sat up, demanding sugar. Yellowish saliva trails covered her chin. Her lips were dry and cracked. Her eyes were still out of focus and almost purple, it seemed to me. Her left cheek was reddened, as if the blood had already started pooling there.

I sketched those marks of death.

I didn't go back to St Martin's for a while. I was offered a commission from a wealthy Frenchwoman and the lure of the money, plus the idea of having my work hang in France, convinced me to take it.

One afternoon, feeling frustrated with the pretty Frenchwoman's face, I pulled out my portrait of Malvika. It made me feel ill to look at it. I had not painted a dead woman before. In the background I had painted a clock, set at 5:37.

I thought of the taxi drivers and how easily they repeated the legend of the disappearing girl. How happily they unconsciously supported their rapist companion. I knew that I would not be able to finish my portrait of Malvika until I knew her as a young girl, traced her steps over and over again.

I began then a week, or was it two? Of catching taxis after five, outside the handicraft centre. I did it a dozen times, maybe more. Some of them told me proudly, "A lot of drivers won't pick up young girls from there. But I don't believe in ghosts."

One evening, the driver said, "You been shopping?" His eyes looked at me in the mirror but not at me. Beside me. I've always found cross-eyed people hard to talk to.

"Yes," I said, though I had no bags.

"You girls going dancing tonight?"

"Girls?"

"You and your friend." He nodded at me. Beside me.

I felt prickles down my right arm, as if someone had leaned close to me. I didn't believe there was anyone there, but I didn't want to look. I shifted nearer to the door, and turned my head.

Nothing. No one.

The driver said something in Hindi.

"I'm sorry, I don't speak Hindi," I said, but he spoke more, pausing now and then as you would in a conversation.

"Your friend is very shy," he said.

We turned up the road to the cemetery, heading for St Martin's. I had to continue, my heart beat with it. We passed the cemetery, pulled into St Martin's. The driver turned around.

"Where…is…your friend?" he shouted. He didn't look like a man who shouted. "Where is she? You pay me."

"Will you wait? I just want to see something."

He shook his head, already driving away as I shut the door. "Where is she? Where is that girl?"

Malvika sucked her fingers at me. "Sugar? Sugar?"

No one had cleaned her up and I could see the marks of death clearly, the yellowish saliva on her chin, the purple color of her eyes. "Have you been away? Out?" I said.

She nodded. "I am that girl," and she smiled at me.

I finished my portrait of Malvika. The paint is very thick because I painted her over and over again; young, old, dead. Young, old dead. I could never decide which face captured her best.

Dead Sea Fruit

I have a collection of baby teeth, sent to me by recovered anorexics from the ward. Their children's teeth, proof that their bodies are working.

One sent me a letter. "Dear Tooth Fairy, you saved me and my womb. My son is now six, here are his baby teeth."

They call the ward Pretty Girl Street. I don't know if the cruelty is intentional; these girls are far from pretty. Skeletal, balding, their breath reeking of hard cheese, they languish on their beds and terrify each other, when they have the strength, with tales of the Ash Mouth Man.

I did not believe the Pretty Girls. The Ash Mouth Man was just a myth to scare each other into being thin. A moral tale against promiscuity. It wouldn't surprise me to hear that the story originated with a group of protective parents, wanting to shelter their children from the disease of kissing.

"He only likes fat girls," Abby said. Her teeth were yellow when she smiled, though she rarely smiled. Abby lay in the bed next to Lori; they compared wrist thickness by stretching their fingers to measure.

"And he watches you for a long time to make sure you're the one," Lori said.

"And only girls who could be beautiful are picked," Melanie said. Her blonde hair fell out in clumps and she kept it in a little bird's nest beside her bed. "He watches you to see if you could be beautiful enough. If you're thinner, then he saunters over to you."

He watches you to see if you are beautiful enough. He only

helps those who will be beautiful when properly thin. If that's you, then he saunters over."

The girls laughed. "He saunters. Yes," they agreed. They trusted me; I listened to them and fixed their teeth for free.

"He didn't saunter," Jane said. I sat on her bed and leaned close to hear. "He beckoned. He did this," and she tilted back her head, miming a glass being poured into her mouth. "I nodded. I love vodka," she said. "Vodka's made of potatoes, so it's like eating."

The girls all laughed. I hate it when they laugh. I have to maintain my smile. I can't flinch in disgust at those bony girls, mouths open, shoulders shaking. All of them exhausted with the effort.

"I've got a friend in New Zealand and she's seen him," Jane said. "He kissed a friend of hers and the weight just dropped off her."

"I know someone in England who kissed him," Lori said.

"He certainly gets around," I said. They looked at each other.

"I was frightened at the thought of him at first," Abby said. "Cos he's like a drug. One kiss and you're hooked. Once he's stuck in the tongue, you're done. You can't turn back."

They'd all heard of him before they kissed him. In their circles, even the dangerous methods of weight loss are worth considering.

I heard the rattle of the dinner trolley riding the corridor to Pretty Girl Street. They fell silent.

Lori whispered, "Kissing him fills your mouth with ash. Like you pick up a beautiful piece of fruit and bite into it. You expect the juice to drip down your chin but you bite into ashes. That's what it's like to kiss him."

Lori closed her eyes. Her dry little tongue snaked out to the corners of her mouth, looking, I guessed, for that imagined juice. I leaned over and dripped a little water on her tongue.

She screwed up her mouth.

"It's only water," I said. "It tastes of nothing."

"It tastes of ashes," she said.

"They were hoping you'd try a bite to eat today, Lori," I said. She shook her head.

"You don't understand," she said. "I can't eat. Everything tastes like ashes. Everything."

The nurse came in with the dinner trolley and fixed all the Pretty Girls' IV feeds. The girls liked to twist the tube, bend it, press an elbow or a bony buttock into it to stop the flow.

"You don't understand," Abby said. "It's like having ashes pumped directly into your blood."

They all started to moan and scream with what energy they could muster. Doctors came in, and other nurses. I didn't like this part, the physicality of the feedings, so I walked away.

I meet many Pretty Girls. Pretty Girls are the ones who will never recover, who still see themselves as ugly and fat even when they don't have the strength to defaecate. These ones the doctors try to fatten up so they don't scare people when laid in their coffins.

The recovering ones never spoke of the Ash Mouth Man. And I did not believe, until Dan entered my surgery, complaining he was unable to kiss women because of the taste of his mouth. I bent close to him and smelt nothing. I found no decay, no gum disease. He turned his face away.

"What is it women say you taste like?" I said.

"They say I taste of ashes."

I blinked at him, thinking of Pretty Girl Street.

"Not cigarette smoke," the girls had all told me. "Ashes."

"I can see no decay or internal reason for any odour," I told Dan.

After work that day I found him waiting for me in his car outside the surgery.

"I'm sorry," he said. "This is ridiculous. But I wondered if you'd like to eat with me." He gestured, lifting food to his mouth. The movement shocked me. It reminded me of what Jane had said, the Ash Mouth Man gesturing a drink to her. It was nonsense and I knew it. Fairytales, any sort of fiction, annoy me. It's all so very convenient, loose ends tucked in and no mystery left unsolved. Life isn't like that. People die unable to lift an arm to wave and there is no reason for it.

I was too tired to say yes. I said, "Could we meet for dinner tomorrow?"

He nodded. "You like food?"

It was a strange question. Who didn't like food? Then the answer came to me. Someone for whom every mouthful tasted of ash.

"Yes, I like food," I said.

"Then I'll cook for you," he said.

He cooked an almost perfect meal, without fuss or mess. He arrived at the table smooth and brown. I wanted to sweep the food off the table and make love to him right there. "You actually like cooking," I said. "It's nothing but a chore for me. I had to feed myself from early on and I hate it."

"You don't want the responsibility," he said. "Don't worry. I'll look after you."

The vegetables were overcooked, I thought. The softness of them felt like rot.

He took a bite and rolled the food around in his mouth.

"You have a very dexterous tongue," I said. He smiled, cheeks full of food, then closed his eyes and went on chewing.

When he swallowed, over a minute later, he took a sip of water then said, "Taste has many layers. You need to work your way through each to get to the base line. Sensational."

I tried keeping food in my mouth but it turned to sludge and slipped down my throat. It was fascinating to watch him eat. Mesmerising. We talked at the table for two hours, then I started to shake.

"I'm tired," I said. "I tend to shake when I'm tired."

"Then you should go home to sleep." He packed a container of food for me to take. His domesticity surprised me; on entering his home, I laughed at the sheer seductiveness of it. Self-help books on the shelf, their spines unbent. Vases full of plastic flowers with a fake perfume.

He walked me to my car and shook my hand, his mouth pinched shut to clearly indicate there would be no kiss.

Weeks passed. We saw each other twice more, chaste, public events that always ended abruptly. Then one Wednesday, I opened the door to my next client and there was Dan.

"It's only me," he said.

My assistant giggled. "I'll go and check the books, shall I?" she said. I nodded. Dan locked the door after her.

"I can't stop thinking about you," he said. "It's all I think about. I can't get any work done."

He stepped towards me and grabbed my shoulders. I tilted my head back to be kissed. He bent to my neck and snuffled. I pulled away.

"What are you doing?" I said. He put his finger on my mouth to shush me. I tried to kiss him but he turned away. I tried again and he twisted his body from me.

"I'm scared of what you'll taste," he said.

"Nothing. I'll taste nothing."

"I don't want to kiss you," he said softly.

Then he pushed me gently onto my dentist's chair. And he stripped me naked and touched every piece of skin, caressed, squeezed, stroked until I called out.

He climbed onto the chair astride me, and keeping his mouth well away, he unzipped his pants. He felt very good. We made too much noise. I hoped my assistant wasn't listening.

Afterwards, he said, "It'll be like that every time. I just know it."

And it was. Even massaging my shoulders, he could make me turn to jelly.

I had never cared so much about kissing outside of my job before but now I needed it. It would prove Dan loved me, that I loved him. It would prove he was not the Ash Mouth Man because his mouth would taste of plums or toothpaste, or of my perfume if he had been kissing my neck.

"You know we get pleasure from kissing because our bodies think we are eating," I said, kissing his fingers.

"Trickery. It's all about trickery," he said.

"Maybe if I smoke a cigarette first. Then my breath will be ashy anyway and I won't be able to taste you."

"Just leave it." He went out, came back the next morning with his lips all bruised and swollen. I did not ask him where he'd been. I watched him outside on the balcony, his mouth open like a dog tasting the air, and I didn't want to know. I had a busy day ahead, clients all through and no time to think. My schizophrenic client tasted yeasty; they always did if they were medicated.

Then I kissed a murderer; he tasted like vegetable waste. Like the crisper in my fridge smells when I've been too busy to empty it. They used to say people who suffered from tuberculosis smelled like wet leaves; his breath was like that but rotten. He had a tooth he wanted me to fix; he'd cracked it on a walnut shell.

"My wife never shelled things properly. Lazy. She didn't care what she ate. Egg shells, olive pits, seafood when she knew I'm allergic. She'd eat anything."

He smiled at me. His teeth were white. Perfect. "And I mean anything." He paused, wanting a reaction from me. I wasn't interested in his sexual activities. I would never discuss what Dan and I did. It was private, and while it remained that way I could be wanton, abandoned.

"She used to get up at night and raid the fridge," the murderer said after he rinsed. I filled his mouth with instruments again. He didn't close his eyes. Most people do. They like to take themselves elsewhere, away from me. No matter how gentle a dentist is, the experience is not pleasant.

My assistant and I glanced at each other.

"Rinse," I said. He did, three times, then sat back. A line of saliva stretched from the bowl to his mouth.

"She was fat. Really fat. But she was always on a diet. I accused her of secretly bingeing and then I caught her at it."

I turned to place the instruments in my autoclave.

"Sleepwalking. She did it in her sleep. She'd eat anything. Raw bacon. Raw mince. Whole slabs of cheese."

People come to me because I remove the nasty taste from their mouths. I'm good at identifying the source. I can tell by the taste of them and what I see in their eyes.

He glanced at my assistant, wanting to talk but under privilege. I said to her, "Could you check our next appointment, please?" and she nodded, understanding.

I picked up a scalpel and held it close to his eye. "You see how sharp it is? So sharp you won't feel it as the blade gently separates the molecules. Sometimes a small slit in the gums releases toxins or tension. You didn't like your wife getting fat?"

"She was disgusting. You should have seen some of the crap she ate."

I looked at him, squinting a little.

"You watched her. You didn't stop her."

"I could've taken a football team in to watch her and she wouldn't have woken up."

I felt I needed a witness to his words and, knowing Dan was in the office above, I pushed the speaker phone extension to connect me to him.

"She ate cat shit. I swear. She picked it off the plate and ate it," the murderer said. I bent over to check the back of his tongue. The smell of vegetable waste turned my stomach.

"What was cat shit doing on a plate?" I asked.

He reddened a little. When I took my fingers out of his mouth he said, "I just wanted to see if she'd eat it. And she did."

"Is she seeking help?" I asked. I wondered what the breath of someone with a sleep disorder would smell like.

"She's being helped by Jesus now," he said. He lowered his eyes. "She ate a bowlful of dishwashing powder with milk. She was still holding the spoon when I found her in the morning."

There was a noise behind me as Dan came into the room. I turned to see he was wearing a white coat. His hands were thrust into the pockets.

"You didn't think to put poisons out of reach?" Dan said. The murderer looked up.

"Sometimes the taste of the mouth, the smell of it, comes from deep within," I said to the murderer. I flicked his solar plexus with my forefinger and he flinched. His smile faltered. I felt courageous.

As he left, I kissed him. I kiss all of my clients, to learn their nature from the taste of their mouths. Virgins are salty, alcoholics sweet. Addicts taste like fake orange juice, the stuff you spoon into a glass then add water.

Dan would not let me kiss him to find out if he tasted of ash.

"Now me," Dan said. He stretched over and kissed the man on the mouth, holding him by the shoulders so he couldn't get away.

The murderer recoiled. I smiled. He wiped his mouth. Scraped his teeth over his tongue.

"See you in six month's time," I said.

I had appointments with the Pretty Girls, and Dan wanted to come with me. He stopped at the ward doorway, staring in. He seemed to fill the space, a door himself.

"It's okay," I said. "You wait there."

Inside, I thought at first Jane was smiling. Her cheeks lifted and her eyes squinted closed. But there was no smile; she scraped her tongue with her teeth. It was an action I knew quite well. Clients trying to scrape the bad taste out of their mouths. They didn't spit or rinse, though, so the action made me feel queasy. I imagined all that buildup behind their teeth. All the scrapings off their tongue.

The girls were in a frenzy. Jane said, "We saw the Ash Mouth Man." But they see so few men in the ward I thought, "Any man could be the Ash Mouth Man to these girls." I tended their mouths, tried to clear away the bad taste. They didn't want me to go. They were jealous of me, thinking I was going to kiss the Ash Mouth Man. Jane kept talking to make me stay longer, though it took her strength away. "My grandmother was kissed by him. She always said to watch out for handsome men, cos their kiss could be a danger. Then she kissed him and wasted away in about five days."

The girls murmured to each other. Five days! That's a record! No one ever goes down in five days.

In the next ward there are Pretty Boys, but not so many of them. They are much quieter than the girls. They sit in their beds and close their eyes most of the day. The ward is thick, hushed. They don't get many visitors and they don't want me as their dentist. They didn't like me to attend them. They bite at me as if I was trying to thrust my fingers down their throats to choke them.

Outside, Dan waited, staring in.

"Do you find those girls attractive?" I said.

"Of course not. They're too skinny. They're sick. I like healthy women. Strong women. That's why I like you so much. You have the self-esteem to let me care for you. Not many women have that."

"Is that true?"

"No. I really like helpless women," he said. But he smiled.

He smelt good to me, clean, with a light flowery aftershave which could seem feminine on another man. He was tall and broad; strong. I watched him lift a car to retrieve a paper I'd rolled onto while parking.

"I could have moved the car," I said, laughing at him.

"No fun in that," he said. He picked me up and carried me indoors.

I quite enjoyed the sense of subjugation. I'd been strong all my life, sorting myself to school when my parents were too busy to care. I could not remember being carried by anyone, and the sensation was a comfort.

Dan introduced me to life outside. Before I met him, I rarely saw daylight; too busy for a frivolous thing like the sun. Home, transport, work, transport, home, all before dawn and after dusk. Dan forced me to go out into the open. He said, "Your skin glows outdoors. Your hair moves in the breeze. You couldn't be more beautiful." So we walked. I really didn't like being out. It seemed like time wasting.

He picked me up from the surgery one sunny Friday and took my hand. "Come for a picnic," he said. "It's a beautiful day."

In my doorway, a stick man was slumped.

"It's the man who killed his wife," I whispered.

The man raised his arm weakly. "Dentist," he rattled. "Dentist, wait!"

"What happened to you? Are you sleepwalking now?" I asked.

"I can't eat. Everything I bite into tastes of ash. I can't eat. I'm starving." He lisped, and I could see that many of his white teeth had fallen out.

"What did you do to me?" he whispered. He fell to his knees. Dan and I stepped around him and walked on. Dan took my hand, carrying a basket full of food between us. It banged against my legs, bruising my shins. We walked to a park and everywhere we went girls jumped at him. He kissed back, shrugging at me as if to say, "Who cares?" I watched them.

"Why do it? Just tell them to go away," I said. They annoyed me, those silly little girls.

"I can't help it. I try not to kiss them but the temptation is too strong. They're always coming after me."

I had seen this.

"Why? I know you're a beautiful looking man, but why do they forget any manners or pride to kiss you?"

I knew this was one of his secrets. One of the things he'd rather I didn't know.

"I don't know, my love. The way I smell? They like my smell."

I looked at him sidelong. "Why did you kiss him? That murderer. Why?"

Dan said nothing. I thought about how well he understood me. The meals he cooked, the massages he gave. The way he didn't flinch from the job I did.

So I didn't confront him. I let his silence sit. But I knew his face at the Pretty Girls ward. I could still feel him fucking me in the car, pulling over into a car park and taking me, after we left the Pretty Girls.

"God, I want to kiss you," he said.

I could smell him, the ash fire warmth of him and I could feel my stomach shrinking. I thought of my favourite cake, its colour leached out and its flavour making my eyes water.

"Kissing isn't everything. We can live without kissing," I said.

"Maybe you can," he said, and he leant forward, his eyes wide, the white parts smudgy, grey. He grabbed my shoulders. I usually loved his strength, the size of him, but I pulled away.

"I don't want to kiss you," I said. I tucked my head under his arm and buried my face into his side. The warm fluffy wool of his jumper tickled my nose and I smothered a sneeze.

"Bless you," he said. He held my chin and lifted my face up. He leant towards me.

He was insistent.

It was a shock, even though I'd expected it. His tongue was fat and seemed to fill my cheeks, the roof of my mouth. My stomach roiled and I tried to pull away but his strong hands held my shoulders till he was done with his kiss.

Then he let me go.

I fell backward, one step, my heels wobbling but keeping me standing. I wiped my mouth. He winked at me and leant forward. His breath smelt sweet, like pineapple juice. His eyes were blue, clear and honest. You'd trust him if you didn't know.

The taste of ash filled my mouth.

Nothing else happened, though. I took a sip of water and it tasted fresh, clean. A look of disappointment flickered on his face before he concealed it. I thought, You like it. You like turning women that way.

I said, "Have you heard of the myth the Pretty Girls have? About the Ash Mouth Man?"

I could see him visibly lifting, growing. Feeling legendary. His cheeks reddened. His face was so expressive I knew what he meant without hearing a word. I couldn't bear to lose him but I could not allow him to make any more Pretty Girls.

I waited till he was fast asleep that night, lying back, mouth open. I sat him forward so he wouldn't choke, took up my scalpel, and with one perfect move I lifted his tongue and cut it out of his mouth.

The History Thief

Three days Alvin lay on the floor of his dusty lounge room before he realized he was no longer anchored to his body. He rose, enjoying the sense of lightness but also feeling deeply sad at the sight of his small, lonely corpse.

He felt as if he had been asleep for a week, dreaming of an unwelcoming place of darkness. He remembered little of his moment of death, but from the look of his body he had choked on a piece of meat. The meal was at his feet. Lamb chops and mashed potato, it was. Some peas on the side.

He tried to sweep the mess up but had no substance. He sat by his body as the sun rose and set. Rose and set. He knew why he was still there, anchored to earth. The same thing had happened to his father; find my body, you little fucker, his father's ghost had told him. Find my bones and bury them well, or I'll haunt you till your eyes bleed and your dick falls off.

His father had not spoken this way alive.

Hurry up, you lazy fucker. Get my bones in the dirt. No last words from his father apart from that. No loving messages. Once the dirt covered him, he was simply gone.

The answering machine didn't flash at Alvin, but no one ever called. No notes under the door saying, "Popped in but you weren't here." There was mail; Alvin could see it through his front window. No junk mail. The little girl at Number One had taken it upon herself to put stickers on all their letterboxes, so the junk mailers didn't even come down their dead end street anymore.

Alvin hoped someone would find him soon. He felt disembodied; this didn't make him laugh.

Alvin's home sat right at the end, with an abandoned house on one side and a vacant lot on the other. The old woman next door died eighteen months earlier, and her children would be fighting over her will for years, Alvin had heard. He didn't expect to have neighbours soon.

Nobody from the police station had called, but then why would they? They'd all thrown in their two dollars, their five, for his farewell present, the TV and universal remote sitting on a stand in his lounge room, showing a football game. As far as they were concerned, he was sitting up with a packet of Cheetos and a six pack of beer, watching daytime television. If they thought of him at all, they imagined him doing nothing. Resting, at last. He'd worked hard at the station. He swept up, wiped the phones with disinfectant, cleaned the bathroom mirrors, emptied the waste paper bins. Whoever was doing it now may think sometimes that Alvin had done a good job, that there were no surprises left behind, no hard jobs left undone, but none of the rest of them would think of him very often, although he'd always laughed at their jokes and had tried to help their cases in small ways.

One time it was the way the armed robbery suspect bent in the edges of his Styrofoam cup. Alvin'd shown the captain, holding the cup out without speaking.

"That yours, Alvin?"

"No, the suspect. I just noticed when I was cleaning out the bin. Folded in. Like they found behind the counter."

"You're right. You are right." The captain reached out to shake his hand but Alvin stepped backwards, banging into a chair and almost tripping. "I haven't been having a wank, Alvin. Hands are clean," the captain said.

"It's my hands," Alvin said. "I don't want you to touch my dirty hands. Sorry. Sorry."

"You did a great job, Alvin. Okay? Good job."

Alvin had backed out of his office, smiling.

He moved from room to room in his house, grounding himself by looking at his familiar objects. The scented candle on his mantlepiece. He'd never lit it, wanting to save it, and he tried to inhale its scent, regretting his caution. The lady who'd given it to him, all the cops called her Mrs. Moffat. She was lovely. Lovely to look at, lovely in her grief, lovely and kind. She made Alvin feel as if he could be a normal person somehow. Such a good mother, so full of anger and grief. Her daughter, only twelve, murdered and found in the filthiest of public toilets. The shame she must have felt, that poor little girl, shame and pain and terror.

Mrs. Moffat's skin was pale, pink, soft. Her hair was a pale red colour, curly around her head like a fine mist.

He looked at his books, thousands of them, mostly crime. He probably knew more about most cases than the cops did. If he'd been taller, and if his parents had been more encouraging, he might have made it.

His kitchen, dusty but clean. Freezer full of meals for one. He really liked them and was sad to think he'd never eat one again.

Nobody found him. Nobody called. He began to enjoy the sensation; the sense of freedom and he discovered he could explore away from home.

He watched Mr. Wallis at Number Three eat his sausages and chips while reading the newspaper. Sauce sopped up with a piece of bread, sauce under the fingernails although the man was usually clean. He had spoken more to Mr. Wallis than to the others. Mr.

Wallis was often outside doing his roses and it was easy to discuss the colour and health of the flowers.

Alvin tried to talk to Mr. Wallis. "Excuse me, Mr. Wallis. Lovely flowers. Lovely. Have you seen me for a while? Think about it. When was the last time you saw me? You should knock on my door, Mr. Wallis. Be a good neighbour. Wonder where I've been and know I've never been missing for more than a few hours in twenty-five years. Go knock on my door and find me, Mr. Wallis. I'm dead," but Mr Wallis didn't react.

He could slip into all of his neighbours' houses. He'd walked past every day for twenty-five years, never been asked inside. If they were out gardening or collecting their mail they'd talk to him. A simple, "Hello, Alvin, off to work?" or "Back from work?" or "Off to do your shopping?"

He would make small comments but the conversations never developed. They would turn away, or they would ask him something too personal. Or the children would appear with their dirty, grabby hands and he would have to move on, politely, nodding and smiling.

Now, he could sit with them as they ate as if he were part of the family. At Number Five, they ate in front of the television. They ate boiled eggs and toast; it looked delicious. Comforting. He didn't feel like he was intruding; he felt as if he belonged.

At Number Seven, he watched as the young girl (what was she? seventeen?) invited her boyfriend in. He didn't watch more than that. He always changed the channel of the TV if that sort of thing happened. He didn't like it. His mother hadn't, his father hadn't, and he didn't.

The children played soccer in the park next to his house and he tried to grab the ball when it flew loose, but it rolled right through his fingers. He hoped one of them would kick wildly, sending the ball into his yard, perhaps through the window. But his hedge was high. His mother had valued her privacy and the idea of people looking in at them from the park or the street upset her.

"No one wants to look at us, Mum. We might as well be invisible. And we're not doing anything interesting. Just sitting here watching TV."

His father harrumphed. "Nothing but rubbish on."

"You and me watching TV, Dad reading the paper. No one cares."

"You don't know people. They're natural sticky beaks. Poking into business which isn't theirs." But of course his mother was describing herself, like a fly on the wall she could be, especially at the hospital where she worked as a cleaner. He hated how intrusive she was in other people's lives. Sometimes she'd note their addresses and wander by their houses, checking up on them.

Stalking, Alvin called it.

"We do our bit," his parents told him when he said he wanted to try for university. "We are public servants. We do the jobs others might not want to do, but we do them to the best of our abilities. That's our place, Alvin, and there is no other for people like us."

His father worked in administration at the local police station and that, at least, meant he saw some interesting things. When it came time for Alvin to leave school, both parents offered to find him work but it was the police station Alvin was keen on. He liked to solve crimes and look at clues. He liked putting things together.

He had tried other part time jobs but always, for some reason, he had been asked to leave. He knew he did his job well; the references they always gave him attested to that.

"If they want to be all touchy feely, that's their problem," his mother told him. "We can't be expected to be like that just because they want us to. If someone is going to judge you because of it then you're better off without them."

Alvin knew it was more than that. He was not a stupid man. He knew that people just didn't like him. That some people glowed with likeability and made people want to be around them and others, like Alvin and his parents, were either ignored or disliked.

He kept trying to make the neighbors hear him, lead them to discover his body, but no one even shivered. He felt desperate, watching his body rot, knowing he should be elsewhere.

But he found he could move a fair distance. He felt light and released, free from fear. He didn't care what people thought of him, didn't care how he looked. Wasn't concerned that people might touch him, steal from him, knock him down.

He travelled around the block and to his local shopping centre, where he watched people rude and polite, honest people and thieves, acts of love and acts of hatred. It surprised him to know all this went on without him.

Each time he returned, he thought perhaps he'd find police and ambulances, that someone at last would miss him.

He took to walking the streets in an attempt to feel alive, part of the living world. Nobody could see him and out of politeness he avoided touching them.

He'd never even kissed a woman. At school, when everyone else was paired up, even the ugly ones, Alvin sat aside. He watched the sweaty hand-holding with disgust. The sloppy kissing in the classroom distracted him from working. "Pay attention, Alvin," the teachers always said, but it was hard with everything going on and no one to help him out.

The only woman he'd ever really thought about kissing was Mrs. Moffat, and that was not possible anymore. He'd been too polite to approach her then.

His mother had always been proud of his manners.

On the third Friday after his death, he went to his favorite bookshop, which specialized in true crime and the paranormal. Entranced by the window display of a new ghost hunter book, he didn't notice the group of teenagers barreling towards him, talking, walking in that high way teenagers have, as if they are floating on air.

He felt the shock of the young man walking right through him like a jolt of electricity. Alvin stepped out of the young man feeling heavy and full of a dull ache. He could see his own reflection, faint and transparent, in the window.

The friends moved on, unaware. The young man stood, dumb-founded.

"Joe! Come on!" they called. The young man tilted his head at them.

"Joe?" he said.

"Come on, Joe!"

Joe stared at them, completely blank. He didn't seem to know who he was, where he was, who they were. Alvin took a step backwards, feeling the footpath on his feet, watching the teenager's rising panic.

He could feel the footpath.

Alvin was solid. He touched the glass window; cold. He touched his own face; just as cold.

The teenagers led Joe away. His arms waved at them. "It's all right, Joe," they said. And every time, he said, "Am I Joe?"

Alvin sat down on a bench. He was filled with Joe. Joe's life and emotions. Strange things like love, lust, joy. Things Alvin had not experienced.

Joe didn't like his younger sister, not at all. She was ten, a smart arse, smarter than him, everybody said so, but all she did was read. Read her books and talked smart to the adults. Her friends were ten like her and ten was boring; Joe could remember it. He liked reading for a while but it's the sort of thing you grow out of when you get a life. Life is too short to read, he said, and his friends said it too. Sometimes he hid her books. She hated that. "Read a new one," he said. "Start another one," but that's not what she wanted, she wanted to read that one. He'd think of other ways to be cruel as she grew older.

He didn't really like being cruel but there was something about it, something good. He wasn't cruel to everyone, only the ones who deserved it. The ones who gave him the shits, the weak ones who cringed. But there was that kid, the one when they were thirteen, you wouldn't forget that kid, you'd hate to have that kid as a son, you'd feel like a failure. Even Joe's own mother said this. She said, "Oh, how must his mother feel?" when the kid walked past, pants all loose and high, picking his nose, his hair greasy, you could almost see imaginary dogs yapping at his heels to make him walk the way he lifted his flat feet like that.

Joe and his friends bullied him and they all knew it was wrong but couldn't help it. Better than ignoring him, they said, but the friends, they'd know. They'd feel the guilt in the future but not Joe, he'd feel nothing.

Alvin felt laughter, felt that sense of hysteria he'd seen in other people. He'd never really laughed, not like that. He didn't get the jokes, they weren't his kind of thing. But this feeling, this bubbling uncontrollable laughter, he would have lived life differently if he'd known that's what you could feel. Joe's friends and he, sitting around, talkingtalkingtalking, every sentence making them laugh harder, with one of the mothers, who was pretty sexy with her big boobs and her smile, she was younger than the other mothers and she liked these boys, she'd shake her head as if to say, "Oh, you boys," as if only they understood, but she knew that made it funnier, she was that kind of mother. Alvin felt the physical reaction Joe had to her, the rush, the desire.

The desire.

Joe carried desire with him, dreamt it. The first kiss came at fifteen, all bluff and blunder, all soft lips and fluttering eyes, holding hands, checking breath. That was Lori Caldwell and he'd liked her for a long time. Not one of those girls you talk to. Those ones are hard to kiss. Alvin thought they were all hard to kiss. Joe and Lori walking home from school together, him taking the long route, every day for a week, those little hand waves goodbye, little winks, then the hands touching and finally, when her parents were out, around the back, leaning up against the slide and swing set she'd had as a kid, it was all rusty and unsafe but her dad never got around to getting rid of it and it was good to hang on, good to swing even when you were fifteen. There, leaning up against the pole, the kiss.

Alvin couldn't breath. He never knew lips were so soft, or that you wouldn't think of germs, that touch could be so gentle and so good.

It wasn't all good, though. Alvin had always slept well, no need to worry, work secure, parents safe and then parents dead and what's the point of worrying. No money worries. Joe worried about school and the future and the size of his dick. Worried about who hated him and who thought he was weak. Worried about his parents divorcing. Worried that his sister was smarter than him. Worried that Lori didn't care about him, that she'd dump him before he dumped her.

And there it was. Alvin felt it physically, a gently broken heart but he felt it in his stomach and his throat. It hurt. Physically hurt not to cry. No one to talk to who wouldn't laugh or give advice Joe didn't want, a deep sense of loneliness, and that Alvin recognized.

He saw masturbation and magazines, secrets behind closed doors. He saw parents who cared, were connected, but out of their depth.

He tasted huge piles of pasta, tomato sauce straight from the bottle.

He saw Batman, Ironman, toys comics movies books t-shirts. These things had never interested Alvin but now he understood, he felt the obsession.

Alvin knew everything there was to know about the young man Joe. Joe remembered nothing. His life began again.

This was the first time Alvin stole history.

The smell of hot chips filled him and he had a great desire to eat a bucketful. He wondered if he could. He stood up, feeling like a teenager, thin and full of life.

As he walked the feeling faded, as did he. But he had been that boy for a few minutes.

He went home, sliding into his house and glancing, as he always did, at his remains. He sat there as night fell and thought about the fact that his mother and father were not waiting to meet him when he died and thought, as he had many times, that they didn't love him as much as they should have.

His mother killed by a drunk driver. "Don't worry, we'll get him," the cops said. The guy had run into her car, sending it spinning into a lamp post. That took all the impact so the driver slid gently to the side of the road, unhurt.

Bystanders rushing to help said he was laughing and the smell of alcohol was so strong they couldn't breathe.

His mother died instantly, though a bystander swore he'd heard her say "Don't forget to take the mince out." Now that Alvin had walked through Joe and taken his history, he understood what must have happened. She had risen through one of the bystanders ("I felt blank. Maybe the shock. I honestly can't remember checking her pulse or anything.") and was momentarily solid.

He and his father had stood, side by side, at his mother's grave.

People tried to comfort them but both recoiled from the physical contact.

Afterwards, they had sat at the kitchen table laden with food delivered by neighbours. Lifting the lids and sniffing, smiling at each other. All that food. "We'll have to buy a freezer," his dad said. It was the last joke the man made; as soon as the family car was returned fixed, he drove it off a bridge, leaving Alvin both carless and parentless.

His father's body was hard to get to. Get me the fuck out of there, Alvin. Move your lazy fucking prick arse, the man swearing more than Alvin thought possible. Fury in him. Nothing about love or his wife, I love my wife, nothing about that. Just find my fucking body.

Alvin didn't need to sleep or eat or shit but sometimes out of habit or nowhere else to go, he'd watch his own body rot into the carpet. He did it to remind himself that he had lived. He'd known what he now stole from others. Though if he was honest he knew this wasn't true. All that his thieving showed him was that he'd wasted his life. He'd done nothing. Felt nothing. It came as a great surprise, because he thought he'd had a life worth living.

He didn't use his occasional corporeality to tell people about his body. He liked the freedom he had, the ability to discover and explore, that he'd never had in life. He liked stealing history. He liked that he took on enough substance to feel again, although it hurt. He went in clean and clear. Came out full of pain and memory.

He did use his moments of form to order a sign installed on his house, "Holy Order of the Silent Nuns." He set up a light machine, timed to show movement in the evening. Those nuns praying or polishing the silver or whatever else people want to imagine nuns do.

It amused him to do this, although he didn't imagine any of his neighbours would come looking for him now. Still, he liked the idea of movement in his house, even if it was illusion.

His house was fully paid for and all his utility payments automatic. His bank account full from his inheritance. They didn't know that at the police station. They didn't realize he didn't need the money, that it was their company and the stories they told, that he liked to be around them and their crime-solving.

He'd only ever helped in small ways. He'd tried the test once but he never told anyone how he'd done because his absolute failure was too embarrassing.

Alvin discovered that he could steal history gently, a hand through a shoulder. This way he'd gather sensations, feelings. If he went to a bar and timed it right he could remember the taste of beer. They'd be dazed for a minute or two and wouldn't remember emptying the glass. If it was food he craved, the person would forget they'd eaten the hot chips or the garlic bread and Alvin would be left, insubstantial but vaguely there, with the taste on his tongue.

When he wanted more substance, he would step right through them as he had with young Joe.

He stole the history of a renowned chef and for a little while knew how to make a soufflé and perfectly roast a tender cut of meat.

He stole the history of a truck driver and knew how to keep awake for many hours, how to make one punch count, how to know which hitchhiker would likely not kill you.

He stole the history of a young woman, because she walked with such confidence he wanted to know what that felt like. He was surprised by her. He expected perhaps lovers, hardline at the office, the feeling of high heels, the sense of success.

He saw murder.

Her name is Alison, but she calls herself Allara. Always has. Alison is for dull girls and she isn't dull, never dull. At five years old she knew she wanted to be rich and that's what she worked towards. She didn't care what she did. She always said that it is the time when you are not working which identifies you properly. A lot of parties. More parties than Alvin imagined anyone could go to, although he'd heard them in the street. Sometimes they'd invite him, a note in the letterbox, 'All welcome' in small letters although he knew it didn't really include him. Once he'd walked as far as the gate, but the sight of all those strangers, the idea of standing amongst them, touching them, made him turn and go back home. Close the windows, turn up the TV, pretend it wasn't happening. Allara doesn't mind parties. She loves them. She loves strangers more than anything else, because you can amuse a stranger easily, they don't know your tricks. She doesn't like long term friends, doesn't like boyfriends. All too needy and demanding.

She likes night time lovers she can leave at dawn. She likes breakfast alone, she likes smoked salmon on wheat toast, likes tea, she hates coffee. She is in control is always in control except that night six days ago and that she will never forget.

She will forget.

This one she met at a nightclub, tall, dark eyes, there's always one in the nightclub who everyone wants and usually Allara doesn't care, she won't work too hard for it but this one walked over the feet of other women to get to her. What did he see in her he wanted? Later, at his house, when he tied her up in a soundproofed room and held a long, thin knife to her thigh, she said, "Did I look like a victim? What?" He'd drugged her, that was clear, and she was furious with herself.

"Most women don't talk at this stage," he said. He went to a cupboard and pulled out a small box. In it, a dozen women's watches.

Maybe more. "I like to know the time," he said.

"Is that supposed to be funny? Are you supposed to be the Terminator or something? It's not actually funny. Predictable, I'd say. Boring." She actually yawned, but Alvin knew how much effort this cost her. She was used to bluffing men who thought they were stronger than her. She was good at it. "What happens if I need to throw up? Whatever you gave me is making me feel sick."

"Just don't."

"It's not something you can stop." Allara began to make vomiting noises. Like her cat. Her cat did this coughing up a hairball.

He looked at her in disgust. His house was very clean, smelt of disinfectant and air purifier. She turned her head to her shoulder as if blocking her mouth.

"All right, go in the toilet," he said. He untied her, holding the knife to her throat. He dragged her to the bathroom. Her hand over her mouth. She stumbled, faked stumbling, faked weakness. He pushed her inside.

She really did vomit; she didn't have to fake that. There were no weapons in the bathroom, not even any glass jars. Only a toilet brush, nestled in a tall silver case.

Dry retching, she scooped vomit toilet water into the silver case. Filled it. She knocked on the door.

"I'm ready," she said quietly. He opened the door cautiously and she threw it, the whole foul thing, right in his face. She only need a second; he covered his face with his hands, grunting, and she kicked up, high into his groin once, hard down on his shin twice, then, when he moved his hands to protect his groin, both thumbs right into his eye sockets. Pulled his ankles, hard, so he landed on his head, dragged him (strong) onto the bed and tied him up so hard his hands would be blue in minutes.

Alvin felt all this, felt the power of it. He'd never done anything like it, never even close, never even stood his ground when someone pushed in front in the bus queue.

Allara left the killer lying on his bed and she went home. She took his watch with her.

Alvin saw why she didn't report him to the police. She had him still tied there. And each day, she'd go and throw more filth on him. She planned to call the police in a day or two. She didn't want him to die. But she wanted him to suffer, to feel this terror, to be sure he was going to die. He lay in shit on a soaking wet mattress and he cried when he saw her, whimpered.

Alvin felt this like a thrill, like a bolt of electricity.

Allara leant against the wall, emptied. She looked at her watch, his watch, as if that would give her some clue, and she pulled out her purse to check her own ID. Alvin thought she was one of the smartest people he'd stolen history from.

Alvin breathed quickly, trying to numb the pain he always felt on exiting a person.

"Are you all right?" she said. She put out her hand to him. If he didn't know, hadn't seen a filth-covered murderer tied to a bed, he would imagine her a sweet person, nothing but goodness.

It was strange to be looked at, spoken to, by the person whose history had made his body solid. It felt wrong, almost like watching himself masturbate.

Still solid, he stepped into a phone booth and called the police station. He asked for Detective King, a man who'd at least noticed him and whose brain he respected.

"I'd like to report a murderer."

She hadn't moved. She looked at her phone as if expecting a familiar name to pop up there. She looked again at her drivers' license, then up and down the street.

Alvin had already faded or he would at least have directed her home.

Reported in the news the next day, Allara would not know what 'Serial Killer Found' meant. Shockwaves through the community. Abhorrence. Relief. Alvin was proud to have played a part. There was no indication the police were looking for Allara.

He loved helping the police, and he started to follow them around. Sometimes Detective King, but sometimes the street police, following without them knowing, learning from them and watching their mistakes.

There was a violent incident, the stabbing of a gay man in an alley at the back of the pub. There were no witnesses but plenty of observers now, sitting in the pub drinking beer.

There were five police in there, notepads out, asking questions. Trying to win the crowd over, get the right words out of them.

"Which of you did it?" one cop said, wanting the easy way out. "Which of you saw something?" They all laughed, and he did too. They walked around the room checking driving licenses, seeing who was who. That was all they'd be able to do unless they had something to go on.

The observers were silent. They didn't like the cops being there. They drank their beers, nudged each other, looked at the cops with eyes half closed. They had drugs in pockets, they had weapons in the toilet, they had things they didn't want known.

Alvin ran his hands through each shoulder until he found the one whose heart beat faster, who tasted blood in the back of his throat. He pressed his shoulder into the man's chest and stole these words:

Killing a faggot isn't murder.

Alvin stepped inside this one and stole his history. He'd picked correctly; freshest was the feeling of the knife plunging into the victim's chest, the sound of it coming out, the quick wipe and where the knife was hidden. There would be evidence in the man's home of homophobia and photos on his phone of other crimes.

Alvin felt a greater sense of self-belief in this man than any other he'd entered. No sense of his own stupidity (why sit in the pub and drink? This pub? Why not drink elsewhere and perhaps come back in a week, when the crime is forgotten?) and a great disdain for the police; they won't catch me I'm smarter than them I don't care how much school they had they won't catch me.

This one had the taste of onions on his breath, his skin was rough. He had three children who he loved with a deep passion and Alvin could see this man would kill for them. Thought he had killed for them, that 'faggots' would destroy their world. He saw that this man (he was Dean) would protect children because he had not been protected. Only his older brother, dead, why take him why take him and leave these others on earth.

Made flesh by this, Alvin said quietly to the police closest to him, "It was the one with the death metal t- shirt. He threw the knife on the roof. His friends will turn on him for the following reasons. One called Pete, he slept with his girlfriend. One called Will, he stole money from him. One called Dylan is a childhood friend. He killed his cat."

The cop wrinkled his brow. "Do I know you? Worked with you? How do you know this stuff?" He reached out. Alvin stepped back into the shadows. He could feel the back of the chair as his legs touched it, but the feeling faded. He loved the sensation.

He could smell the perfume of the women around him and it made him think of Allara. He wondered if she was at home, all right, wished he could see her. He wished he'd known her as a live person because she seemed kind, as kind as Mrs. Moffat, and she was strong and would help him clean out his house. Sort out his father's clothes, his mother's crockery. She'd help him make the house nice to live in.

She wouldn't, though. He knew that. He knew now how people behaved, and that the only way she'd notice him was in pity.

Word spread of Alvin. He hung around the cops and sometimes they'd call for him, although none of them recognized him. He liked solving the crimes.

He didn't want to steal the history of the old man. Not that old, sixty-five, but old enough. Suspected of a series of rapes, granny rapes they were called but most of the women were true loners, no family. No grandchildren. Most of them had to call police themselves, get themselves an ambulance. Most of them had nobody. This old man, Billy, one of a dozen or more suspects.

Alvin liked leaving the guilty blank, although regretted that this meant they couldn't feel the guilt.

He made sure the police understood the consequences of stealing history. "You realise they will no longer remember, once I've taken it? You gotta be damn sure he's guilty. Once I suck the history, he's not getting it back."

"That's all right. We'll work around it." They all began to understand that he wasn't always there, couldn't always be seen. But they had worked with psychics in the past and this, this was just another variation.

The hardest part was following through with the information. Because he was them, he felt them, and it seemed as if he was turning himself in.

Alvin thought that if Billy was guilty, he shouldn't be allowed the release that taking his history would give him, but the man didn't feel guilt anyway. Alvin didn't want this history, but the police convinced him. "We need him. We need this guy done for. You can help us."

And he did. Saw what others couldn't see and the grannies were safe. There was always evidence, things left behind. There were always frightened people who could be more frightened by someone bigger and scarier.

Calls himself Billy, always did, makes people feel friendly towards you, name like that, makes them think you never quite grew up and you're childlike boylike a lotta fun with a good sense of humour. But they don't laugh at even your best jokes they just smile with that vague old lady smile which is supposed to be polite but is rude as all fuck, rude as all fuck smiling at me when you don't mean it.

He's Billy but he's also William, working quiet in the corner, 35 years in the office and no one comes to him for the corporate knowledge, do they? No one asks him what he knows until the day he retires and they send him off as if surprised he's still there. They don't know what's inside his head. He's seen every last one of them stripped naked begging for it. Male and female, they're all begging for it and he's the one to help them. Good things come in quiet packages and they know it, begging for it.

The ones begging the hardest are the old ladies. All done up with their nice shoes bought 40 years ago and their coats reeking of moth balls because they don't think a coat needs cleaning, not when you just wear it shopping every day for a hundred years. Stockings, the brown stockings, that's what gets him going and he could never tell you why but pinching the nylon of the thigh? Squeezing it up and then getting the fingernails in and tearing? Don't get me started do get me started I'm started just thinking about it.

Detective King shook Alvin's hand gently. "I'm still a bit concerned we can see you like this. Just for a little while. But you're doing good work. Very, very good work."

"That wasn't too pleasant."

"Think nice thoughts. Think about pretty things. That's what I do. Dandelion heads. Smell of peach blossom. Taste of mango. Think of that kind of thing."

"Sometimes I think of Mrs. Moffat. Remember her?" Alvin felt breathless. He didn't usually make such honest statements.

"We all remember her. Lovely lady. Tragic. Tragic. That husband of hers still locked up, you know. She's still on her lonesome, far as we know. Couple of us keep track, make sure she's okay, you know? Tragic life. Tragic."

Some nights he struggled to keep all the history separate. Parts of it he forgot, but some he would remember forever. The suck of history is always stronger in the place it happened. Alvin learnt to smell it in the air, hear the echo.

Sometimes on these confusing nights he would wander, looking for Allara. He knew where she lived; he remembered that from being her. But she was no longer there and he wondered if she had made it home. It made him even lonelier, thinking of her.

His body became sludge, then bones. The imaginary nuns were left alone and he managed to collect his mail when he was flesh. Each day, like a real job, he went to the police station.

He loved taking history. Live the lives he never lived. Though sometimes he tired of stealing the history of the guilty and wanted innocent history.

He entered Number Eight, a house full of noise and light. He'd never dared speak to them because they seemed so enclosed, so happy. They had a lot of friends and he wasn't one of them. He took the history of the son, a surprising history of cruelty to animals, a fascination with blood.

Miss Evans is so mean and she hates me. Mum thinks she is just young and getting used to the kids but she hates me and Mum isn't on my side. She told the principal and the principal said I had to be better behaved but this Miss Evans is the one. If I make her sad she might be nicer. If I kill her cat she will be nicer and if I let her know it was me she will hate me even more but if I'm nice to her about her cat and give her a card with a cat on it to make her cry she won't hate me any more.

Alvin felt sadness, that there was no innocence in the world. He had lived a life so protected. He wondered if he should approach Miss Evans, who clearly had some pain ahead of her, but decided against it. It was not his business. Not his concern.

Back in his home, he stared at the candle, one glowing item in his dark house, lit or not. He thought of her, Mrs. Moffat. He wasn't alone in finding her delightful. The other cops made jokes (were they jokes? Alvin passed his arm through a shoulder and discovered; no. serious) that they would go comfort her in her long time of loneliness. She didn't even have her father now; he'd been placed in an old people's home.

If there was one thing Alvin had learnt, it was that the subtle approach could work. She'd think he was crazy if he appeared before her, slavering. This way he could watch her at her best, with her father.

He knew he could have followed her everywhere, watched her at her daily activities but he would not do that. That was not the sort of person he was. She might come to know him and perhaps he could stay with her sometimes, sit in her loungeroom while she stuffed envelopes for charity. Cooked for new parents. All the things he was sure she did.

He waited, instead, in the foyer of the home her father lived in. Sat and waited, invisible in the chair near the harsh-voiced receptionist, watching the comings and goings.

A visit to an old person's home was ripe with possibility, full of history. Leaving them lost for thought and diagnosed with Alzheimer's. Alvin sometimes wondered how many sufferers were that way because their history had been stolen. It crossed his mind.

Alvin didn't take much of them after a while because sometimes the memories were tattered. Hard to tell truth from false memory.

The older they were, the scratchier the history. He knew he had to get them before the history started to disintegrate.

When he had a body, he could smell when the history had turned. Women in particular took on a greasy scent once they become of a certain age. Once they passed the age of procreation, they lost their sensual allure.

There were perfumes developed to cover this up. To counteract the nasty smell of history rotting on the breath.

He watched the innocence of old age. Old faces look innocent. Lines of age hiding all other clues. They could have done anything, these people, but now all they were was old.

He didn't care or think of the fact that history was lost once he stole it. He forgot the stories, usually, and the stories were lost to them. All their experiences, all the things that justified a life.

He heard people say that Mrs. Moffat's father was the last living person to have seen Dame Nellie Melba perform. He was five when he saw her sing and always his favourite dessert was Peach Melba. He would never taste it again.

Quiet and unseen, Alvin watched as Mrs. Moffat arrived. Followed her to her father's small mauve room.

"Oh, Dad, look at you getting spoiled. You're a lucky man, aren't you? Look at you all pleased with yourself."

"It's all slipping away from him, though. Life is cruel." The nurse said this to herself, plumping the pillows and patting the old man's head. "He's a dear one. Always a smile."

"He always did have a smile for others," Mrs. Moffat said. Alvin was surprised to hear the tone of her voice, the bitterness. He felt even closer to her, two people with parents not loving enough.

"I'll leave you to it then. I see you've brought some cakes for him. Any leftovers gratefully received!" the nurse said, patting her fat stomach and smiling.

Mrs. Moffat took a cake and ate it. Her father reached out, "One for me, love, I love a cake."

"Nothing for you," she whispered. They sat in silence for ten minutes, a long, drawn-out painful time.

"Tell me about Georgia. How's my dear little granddaughter?"

"Dead, Dad. Don't you remember? She was twelve. We'd just celebrated her twelfth birthday, out at a Japanese restaurant but she wouldn't eat anything. You know what she was like, fussy as anything."

"You were fussy," he said, smiling. "Wouldn't eat your greens no matter how we threatened you."

"She's much fussier. It has to be all one colour or she won't touch it. She chose the restaurant and still she won't even eat it. You know? The nine of us sitting there, six of her dull little friends, and Mark, and the girls giggling at me as if I'm a fool. They have no idea. They are jealous of how I look, I know that much. She was supposed to walk straight home from school but most days it takes her close to an hour. Gossiping. Dawdling. Me sitting at home worrying about her. They say her father picked up her that day, Dad. Can you imagine? Mark leaving work early to pick her up? That's what they say happened. They say he drove her to the park and stopped there. I'd never let her go there. Teenagers hang out drinking and smoking, it's full of glass, full of crap and influence and there's a bad feeling there. I always felt as if she'd be raped there and I told her that, I terrified her about that place so she'd never go near it. Even the mention of it made her close her eyes so imagine how she felt when her father drove her there.

"They say he first of all made her take her clothes off, and that he cut her with something sharp along her arms and legs. They say he gave her something in a drink, to make her sleepy, but she still felt pain. A lot of pain. He raped her (Why? Why? He got plenty from me and from his girlfriends as if I didn't know about them) and then he called in the teenagers and they raped her too, and they beat her cut her, they poured things on her and they left her in the toilet to die."

They were both crying now.

"He wouldn't. He couldn't."

"He did, Dad. All the evidence pointed to him. Every last bit and they looked hard."

"I wish we knew for sure."

"I wish we did, too."

"If we knew for sure I'd spend my last breath to get him."

Crying open mouthed, they looked very much father and daughter.

Alvin wanted to feel what they felt. He brushed gently against the old man, just to get the feeling. Just to get a voice.

"'Such an emotional time," the nurse said as Mrs. Moffat handed over the cakes.

The old man seemed to be empty of anything but grief. While Mrs. Moffat was in the hallway, Alvin, solid in voice alone, said in his ear, "I can help you forget. I can suck out your history and tell it back to you and you won't even notice."

"Go for it, son. You do it." Alvin thought knowing the father would help him know the daughter, and he stepped inside.

It was dark and ragged. A mind unraveling. The granddaughter,

Georgia, she was sweet and loving and funny. Safe. She was always safe and trusting because she had never been hurt, never been lost or lonely or discarded. His childhood, that was clearer than anything else. Barefeet, tough as old nails, fingers strong from helping with the dairy cows, his mother calling, "Breakfast" and the smell of bacon and fresh porridge.

The rest was sorrow.

"Alvin?" Mrs. Moffat said, standing in the doorway. "Alvin? From the police station? It's me, Dana! Dana Moffat! What…are you doing with my father? Where did you come from? You always were a quiet one."

Alvin, made flesh but only just, felt tears, real tears, that she knew who he was.

"Dad?" she said. She stepped forward, stared into the man's eyes. He smiled, simple, empty.

"What did you do?" she asked Alvin.

"I can steal the history. Know them. I can know the truth."

"Truth is important," she said. "But what do you mean?"

"He grew up on a dairy farm. He loved you very much until he sometimes forgets who you are. He cannot believe his granddaughter is dead because those things don't happen in his family. But he has peace now. He remembers nothing."

He felt himself fading. "Can I come to see you?" he said before it became too strange.

She nodded. Weeping.

Alvin couldn't bear hearing her in pain. She had been kind to him. Noticed him and once she brought him a gift, the small scented candle which he kept on his mantelpiece and had never lit. He always cleaned the arms of the chair before she sat down, made sure everything was nice for her. One time, she'd touched his shoulder, which almost hurt. His family had been so physically distant he hated anything physical now. All of them had sensitive skin but his father made it his mother's fault.

"Frigid, you are, and your son, too. Pity his poor bride," he'd say. "You'll be wearing gloves, I imagine. Won't ever know the touch of a soft, white thigh."

He wanted to talk to Mrs. Moffat again desperately. He had stolen history simply to become flesh before, but this time he took three lives and was so solid he could open doors. Every time he did it, he grew larger. Thicker. He was a tub of gasses and pain, bloated on other people's history.

He knocked at her front door.

"Oh, you came, Alvin. You said you would and you did. Did you come from work?"

He loved the fact he could smell the fresh-cut flowers on her kitchen bench, and the coffee she brewed.

"I retired."

"So young?" She smiled at him, offered him coffee, but he didn't think he had enough flesh.

He knew he had to speak quickly.

"Listen to me," he said, and he told her what he could do, that he could take her husband's mind, be sure of his guilt. "I'll tell you what I tell the police. It will be lost. He will no longer have that history so can't feel guilty about it," he said.

"You'll know for sure? I don't know if I want that. What would we do?" Her cheeks were flushed.

She seemed unaware of the affect she had on them all. She was one of those people, Alvin thought, who people wanted to be around. He didn't really know what the difference was between her and his own mother. She was prettier, of course, and she smiled a lot. And she touched people. And she looked them in the eye and blinked, pretty sweet blinks which broke your heart.

"Some of the police think that he should be killed. An accident or something. But I don't think anyone should die like that." She shook her head.

"If you were sure of what he'd done, you would feel differently perhaps."

"I could never be sure. I love him…loved him. But things have changed. I've spoken to so many people about the masks we carry. Men like him, they can carry a mask so that even they are convinced. If I knew he did it I'd…"

"You could do it. You could shoot him."

He felt himself fading, and she looked at him oddly. "Alvin, I…I can see through you."

"I'll come back," he said. He walked to the street, took three more histories and returned to tell her the truth.

"I'm not always flesh, Mrs. Moffat. I am mostly ghost. My remains are in my house. I don't want to shock you," although she seemed barely shocked. "I have to stay around as long as my remains are unburied. But I don't mind. I like it here. I like helping people. And I'm scared of what comes next. I don't want to leave here."

She smiled at him. "You're a good man. You always were."

Alvin began to fade.

"You'll come back soon? Talk about this some more? Come back tomorrow. Or I could come to you."

Alvin felt a moment of pride to think of his neighbors seeing a woman as beautiful as Mrs. Moffat entering his house. But no. She shouldn't be seen.

"Don't park in the street. You can enter through the vacant lot, from the other side."

"You really are a natural at this," she said.

"If I can read your husband for his innocence, he'll be released. But he will no longer know you. He'll no longer know anything."

"He doesn't know anything now."

"You don't know what's hidden in a man."

"What if you find out he's guilty?"

"What do you think?"

"If he's guilty, I would hate him to death. I would hate him more than any human being."

"Then we will decide once I know." Alvin did not tell her what else motivated him, that perhaps, if he understood her husband, knew the man she loved, that he could imitate him.

Alvin knew that Mrs. Moffat wanted him to go ahead, but perhaps she didn't want the responsibility. So early on Monday, he visited the jail. He would surprise her with the information.

Her husband was a popular man. People said gracious. No matter how hard anyone pushed, he didn't answer. "Who killed her then? Who killed your daughter?" but the question only made him quieter.

He was a silver-haired man. His voice was gentle, but the newspapers said they saw a glint in his eye. In jail he seemed reasonably well respected. He shared all he had, helped the others, had no testosterone, unattractive and too old for them to want to rape. Alvin looked forward to stealing his history, understanding him. Because this was the man Mrs. Moffat loved.

Alvin had no substance as he moved closer, but still the man turned on Alvin's approach. Alvin stepped into him and stole his history.

The newest stuff was the freshest and that hurt; jail time, cold and frightening. A few good men, most of them okay, most of them believing him and that felt good, he wasn't used to that. Hunger; that hunger when you can't feed yourself, you have to eat what's given whether you like it or not. A constant ache inside; Alvin hadn't felt this before but he realized it was loss, an empty space where a child should go. Then worse than that. A darkness, a torturous sadness, terrible grief, but what was missing was guilt. No guilt about daughter's death. No violence. Nothing but grief. Not even any knowledge of who had killed her. There was Mrs. Moffat with her pretty face but harder, just a little bit harder in this man's history but who isn't, who doesn't get sharper when you know them better, who isn't more layered than first viewing?

The man was innocent.

Alvin thought, They planted evidence. That's what they do.

The man sat on his bed, staring at the wall. A small smile on his face; relief, perhaps. Emptiness being greater than grief. Alvin was too solid to move through the door and he squatted in the corner, terrified. He hadn't thought of this, that he would be locked up. He didn't want to learn the histories of the other prisoners. He didn't want to know that stuff; there with all the child molesters.

Alvin felt a strange tugging, and he smelt something like dirt. He wanted to race to find Mrs. Moffat, at the old people's home, or at her home, but this was like a magnet, drawing him, dragging him home. As he approached he stole the history of a motorist, stopped with a broken car. Made substance and head full of math, recriminations, two cute kids and a memory of peppermint ice-cream, Alvin physically opened his own front door.

The first thing he noticed was that his remains were gone. And that the scented candle was lit.

He touched the dark stain on the carpet where he had rested. The tug pulled him harder, into the backyard, and there was Mrs. Moffat, spading dirt into a hole.

He felt blurry, very blurry.

She looked up as he approached.

"Not much of you," she said. "In spirit nor in bone. I thought I would help you move on, now we know the truth."

"I don't want to move on," he said. "I'm happy." But he wasn't happy, now. Knowing the truth. "He didn't do it. Your husband is innocent. He's as sad as you are."

"Is he? And does he think he knows who did kill our dear little precious?" She spat these last words. Kept on spading dirt.

"Please, please stop burying me."

"No, Alvin. It's time for you to go. Your truth and my truth don't really match. And the only two people who know me well enough have been wiped clean."

She stamped down on his grave and began a short prayer.

Alvin reached for her but he had little strength to take much. Just a deep, irrational hatred for her husband. A sense of victory at her mother's death. And the smell of blood and the terrified begging of her trusting young daughter.

The Gaze Dogs of Nine Waterfall

Rare dog breeds; people will kill for them. I've seen it. One stark-nosed curly hair terrier, over-doped and past all use. One ripped-off buyer, one cheating seller. I was just the go-between for that job. I shrank up small into the corner, squeezed my eyes shut, folded my ears over like a Puffin Dog, to keep the dust out.

I sniffed out a window, up and out, while the blood was still spilling. It was a lesson to me, early on, to always check the dog myself.

I called my client on his cell, confirming the details before taking the job.

"Ah, Rosie McDonald! I've heard good things about your husband."

I always have to prove myself. Woman in a man's world. I say I'm acting for my husband and I tell stories about how awful he is, just for the sympathy.

I'll bruise my own eye, not with make-up. Show up with an arm in a sling. "Some men don't like a woman who can do business," I say. "But he's good at what he does. An eye for detail. You need that when you're dealing dogs."

"I heard that. My friend is the one who was after a Lancashire Large. For his wife."

I remembered; the man had sent me pictures. Why would he send me pictures?

"He says it was a job well done. So you know what I'm after?"

"You're after a vampire dog. Very hard to locate. Nocturnal, you know? Skittish with light. My husband will need a lot of equipment."

"So you'll catch them in the day when they're asleep. I don't care about the money. I want one of those dogs."

"My husband is curious to know why you'd like one. It helps him in the process."

"Doesn't he talk?"

"He's not good with people. He's good at plenty, but not people."

"Anyway, about the dog: thing is, my son's not well. It's a blood thing. It's hard to explain even with a medical degree."

My ears ring when someone's lying to me. Even over the phone. I knew he was a doctor; I'd looked him up.

"What's your son's name?"

The silence was momentary, but enough to confirm my doubts there was a son. "Raphael," he said. "Sick little Raphael." He paused. "And I want to use the dog like a leech. You know? The blood-letting cure."

"So you just need the one?"

"Could he get more?"

"He could manage three, but your son…"

"Get me three," he said.

I thought, Clinic. $5,000 each. Clients in the waiting room reading *Nature* magazine. All ready to have their toxins sucked out by a cute little vampire dog. I decided to double my asking price, right there.

There are dogs rare because of the numbers. Some because of what they are or what they can do.

And some are rare because they are not always seen.

I remember every animal I've captured, but not all of my clients. I like to forget them. If I don't know their faces I can't remember their expressions or their intent.

The Calalburun. I traveled to Turkey for this puppy. Outside of their birthplace, they don't thrive, these dogs. There is something about the hunting in Turkey which is good for them. My client wanted this dog because it has a split nose. Entrancing to look at. Like two noses grown together.

The Puffin Dog, or Norwegian Lundehound. These dogs were close to extinction when a dog-lover discovered a group of them on a small island. He bred them up from five, then shared some with an enthusiast in America. Not long after that, the European dogs were wiped out, leaving the American dogs the last remaining.

The American sent a breeding pair and some pups back to Europe, not long before her own dogs were wiped out. From those four there are now about a thousand.

The dogs were bred to hunt puffins. They are so flexible (because they sometimes needed to crawl through caves to hunt) that the back of their head can touch their spine. As a breed, though, they don't absorb nutrients well, so they die easily and die young. We have a network, the other dealers and I. Our clients want different things at different times so we help each other out. My associate in Europe knew of four Puffin Dogs.

It's not up to me to ponder why people keep these cripples alive. Animal protection around the world doesn't like it much; I just heard that the English RSPCA no longer supports Crufts Dog Show because they say there are too many disabled dogs being bred and shown. Dogs like the Cavalier King Charles Spaniel, whose skull is too small for its brain. And a lot of boxer dogs are prone to epilepsy, and some bulldogs are unable to mate, or are unable to give birth unassisted.

It's looks over health. But humans? Same same.

The Basenji is a dog which yodels. My client liked the sound and wanted to be yodeled to. I don't know how that worked out.

Tea cup dogs aren't registered and are so fragile they need to be carried everywhere. Some say this is the breeders' way of selling off runts.

Then there's the other dogs. The Black Dogs, Yellow Dogs, the Sulphurous Beast, the Wide-Eyed Hound, the Wisht Hound, and the Hateful Thing: The Gabriel Hound.

I've never been asked to catch one of these, nor have I seen one, but god-awful stories are told.

The only known habitat of the vampire dog is the island of Viti Levu, Fiji. I'd never been there but I'd heard others talk of the rich pickings. I did as much groundwork as I could over the phone, then visited the client to get a look at him and pick up the money. No paper trail. I wore tight jeans with a tear across the ass and a pink button up shirt.

He was ordinary; they usually are. The ones with a lot of money are always confident but this one seemed overly so. Stolen riches? I wondered. The ones who get rich by stealing think they can get away with everything. Two heads taller then me, he wore a tight blue t-shirt, blank. A rare thing; most people like to plaster jokes on their chests. He didn't shake my hand but looked behind me for the real person, my husband.

"I'm sorry, my husband was taken ill. He's told me exactly what I need to do, though," I said.

The client put his hand on my shoulder and squeezed. "He's lucky he's got someone reliable to do his dirty work," the guy said.

He gave me a glass of orange soda as if I were a child. That's fine; making money is making money.

I told him we'd found some dogs, but not for sale. They'd have to be caught and that would take a lot more.

"Whatever… Look, I've got a place to keep them."

He showed me into his backyard, where he had dug a deep hole. Damp. The sides smooth, slippery with mud. One push and I'd be in there.

I stepped back from the edge.

"So, four dogs?" he said. "Ask your husband if he can get me four vampire dogs."

"I will check."

It was a year since my husband Joe had his spine bitten half out by a glandular-affected bulldog, and all he could do was nod, nod, nod. Bobble head, I'd call him if I were a cruel person. I had him in an old people's home where people called him young man and used his tight fists to hold playing cards. When I visit, his eyes follow me adoringly, as if he were a puppy.

My real hunting partner was my sister-in-law Gina. She's an animal psychologist. An animal psychic, too, but we don't talk about that much. I pretend I don't believe in it, but I rely on the woman's instincts.

The job wouldn't be easy, but it never is in the world of the rare breed.

My bank account full, our husband and brother safe with a good stock of peppermints, Gina and I boarded a flight for Nadi, Fiji. Ten hours from LA, long enough to read a book, snooze, maybe meet a dog-lover or two. We transferred to the Suva flight, a plane so small I thought a child could fly it. They gave us fake orange juice and then the flight was done. I listened to people talk, about local politics, gossip. I listened for clues, because you never knew when you'll hear the right word.

Gina rested. She was keen to come to Fiji, thinking of deserted islands, sands, fruit juice with vodka.

The heat as we stepped off the plane was like a blanket had been thrown over our heads. I couldn't breathe in it and my whole body steamed sweat. It was busy but not crazy, and you weren't attacked by cabbies looking for business, porters, jewellery sellers. I got a lot of smiles and nods.

We took a cab which would not have passed inspection in New York and he drove us to our hotel on Suva Bay. There were stray dogs everywhere, flaccid, unhealthy looking things. The females had teats to the ground, the pups were mangy and unsteady. They didn't seem aggressive, though. Too hot, perhaps. I bought some cut pineapple from a man at the side of the road and I ate it standing there, the juice dripping off my chin and pooling at my feet. I bought another piece, and another, and then he didn't have any change so I gave him twenty dollars. Gina couldn't eat; she said the dogs put her off. That there was too much sickness.

I didn't sleep well. I felt slick with all the coconut milk I'd had with dinner; with the fish, with the greens, with the dessert. And new noises in a place keep me awake, or they entered my dreams in strange ways.

I got up as the sun rose and swam some laps. The water was warm, almost like bath water, and I had the pool to myself.

After breakfast, Gina and I took a taxi out to the latest sighting of vampire dogs, a farm two hours drive inland. I like to let the locals drive. They know where they're going and I can absorb the landscape and listen while they tell me stories.

The foliage thickened as we drove, dark leaves waving heavily in what seemed to me a still day. The road was muddy so I had to be patient; driving through puddles at speed can get you bogged. A couple of trucks passed us. Smallish covered vehicles with the stoutest workers in the back. They waved and smiled at me and I knew that four of them could lift our car out of the mud if we got stuck.

The trucks swerved and tilted and I thought that only faith was keeping them on the road.

The farm fielded dairy cows and taro. It seemed prosperous; there was a letter box rather than an old juice bottle, and white painted rocks lined the path.

There was no phone here, so I hadn't been able to call ahead. Usually I'd gain permission to enter, but that could take weeks, and I wanted to get on with the job.

I told the taxi driver to wait. A fetid smell filled the car; rotting flesh.

"Oh, Jesus," Gina said. "I think I'll wait, too." I saw a pile of dead animals at the side of a dilapidated shed; a cow, a cat, two mongooses. They could've been there since the attack a week ago.

"Wait there," I told Gina. "I'll call you if I need you."

Breathing through my mouth, I walked to the pile. I could see bite marks on the cow and all the animals appeared to be bloodless, sunken.

"You are who?" I heard. An old Fijian woman wearing a faded green t-shirt that said "Nurses know better" pointed at me. She looked startled. They didn't see many white people out here.

"Are you from the Fiji Times?" she said. "We already talked to them."

I considered for a moment how best to get the information. She seemed suspicious of the newsmakers, tired of them.

"No, I'm from the SPCA. I'm here to inspect the animals and see if we can help you with some money. If there is a person hurting the animals, we need to find that person and punish them."

"It's not a person. It is the vampire dogs. I saw them with my own eyes."

"This was done by dogs?"

She nodded. "A pack of them. They come out of there barking and yelping with hunger, and they run here and there sucking their food out of any creature they find. They travel a long way sometimes, for new blood."

"So they live in the hills?" I thought she'd pointed at the mountains in the background. When she nodded, I realized my mistake. I should have said, "Where do they live?"

It was too late now; she knew what she thought I wanted to hear.

"They live in the hills."

"Doesn't anyone try to stop them?"

"They don't stop good. They are hot to the touch and if you get too near you might burn up."

"Shooting?"

"No guns. Who has a gun these days?"

"What about a club, or a spear? What about a cane knife? What I mean is, can they be killed?"

"Of course they can be killed. They're dogs, not ghosts."

"Do they bite people?"

She nodded. "If they can get close enough?"

"Have they killed anyone? Or turned anyone into a vampire?"

She laughed, a big, belching laugh, which brought tears to her eyes. "A person can't turn into a vampire dog! If they bite you, you clean out the wound so it doesn't go nasty. That's all. If they suck for long enough you'll die. But you clean it out and it's okay."

"So what did they look like?"

She stared at me.

"Were they big dogs or small?" I measured with my hand, up and down until she grunted; knee high.

"Fur? What color fur?"

"No fur. Just skin. Blue skin. Loose and wrinkly."

"Ears? What were their ears like?"

She held her fingers up to her head. "Like this."

"And they latched onto your animals and sucked their blood?"

"Yes. I didn't know at first. I thought they were just biting. I tried to shoo them. I took a big stick and poked them. Their bellies. I could hear something sloshing away in there."

She shivered. "Then one of them lifted its head and I saw how red its teeth were. And the teeth were sharp, two rows atop and bottom, so many teeth. I ran inside to get my husband but he had too much kava. He wouldn't even sit up."

"Can I see what they did?" I said. The woman looked at me.

"You want to see the dead ones? The bokola?"

"I do. It might help your claim."

"My claim?"

"You know, the SPCA." I walked back to the shed.

Their bellies had been ripped out and devoured and the blood drained, she'd said.

There were bite marks, purplish, all over their backs and legs, as if the attacking dogs were seeking a good spot.

The insects and the birds had worked on the ears and other soft bits.

I took a stick to shift them around a bit.

"The dogs will come for those bokola. You leave them alone." She waved at the pile of corpses.

"The dogs?"

"Clean-up dogs. First the vampires, then the clean-up. Their yellow master sends them."

"Yellow master?" She shook her head, squeezed her eyes shut. Taboo subject.

"You wouldn't eat this meat? It seems a waste."

"The vampire dogs leave a taste behind," the woman told me. "A kamikamica taste the other animals like. One of the men in my village cooked and ate one of those cows. He said it made him feel very good but now he smells of cowhide. He can't get the smell off himself."

"Are any of your animals left alive?"

The woman shook her head. "Not the bitten ones. They didn't touch them all, though."

"Can I see the others?" I would look for signs of disease, something to explain the sudden death. I wanted to be sure I was in the right place.

One cow was up against the back wall of the house, leaning close to catch the shade. There was a sheen of sweat on my body. I could feel it drip down my back.

"Kata kata," the woman said, pointing to the cow. "She is very hot."

It looked all right, apart from that.

I could get no more out of her.

Gina was sweating in the taxi. It was a hot day, but she felt the heat of the cow as well. "Any luck?" she said.

"Some. There's a few local taboos I'll need to get through to get the info we need, though."

"Ask him," she said, pointing at the driver. "He's Hindi."

Our taxi driver said, "I could have saved you the journey. No Fijian will talk about that. We Hindis know about those dogs."

He told us the vampire dogs lived at the bottom of Ciwa Waidekeulu. "Thiwa Why Ndeke Ulu," he said. Nine Waterfall. In the rainforest twenty minutes from where we were staying.

"She said something about a yellow master?"

"A great yellow dog, worse than the worst man you've ever met."

I didn't tell him I'd met some bad men.

"You should keep away from him. He can give great boons to the successful, but there is no one successful. No one can defeat the yellow dog. Those who fail will vanish, as if they have never been." He stopped at a jetty, where some children sold us roti filled with a soft, sweet potato curry. Very, very good.

The girl who cleaned my room was not chatty at first, but I wanted to ask her questions. She answered most of them happily once I gave her a can of Coke. "Where do I park near Ciwa Waidekeulu? How do I ask the Chief for permission to enter? Is there fresh water?"

When I asked her if she knew if the vampire dogs were down there, she went back to her housework, cleaning an already-spotless bench. "These are not creatures to be captured," she said. "They should be poisoned." To distract me, she told me that her neighbours had five dogs, every last one of them a mongrel, barking all night and scaring her children. I know what I'd do if I were her. The council puts out notices of dog poisonings, Keep Your Dogs in While We Kill the Strays, so all she'd have to do is let their dogs out while the cull was happening. Those dogs'd be happy to run; they used to leap the fence, tearing their guts, until her neighbour built his fence higher. They're desperate to get out.

They do a good job with the poisoning, she told me, but not so good with the clean up. Bloated bodies line the streets, float down the river, clog the drains.

They don't understand about repercussions, and that things don't just go away.

The client was pleased with my progress when I called him. "So, when will you go in?"

With the land taboo, I needed permission from the local chief or risk trouble. This took time. Most didn't want to discuss the vampire dogs, or the yellow dog king; he was forbidden, also. "It may be a couple of weeks. Depends on how I manage to deal with the locals."

"Surely a man would manage better," he said. "I know your husband doesn't like to talk, but most men will listen to a man better. Maybe I should send someone else."

"Listen," I told him, hoping to win him back, "I've heard they run with a fat cock of a dog. Have you heard that? People have seen the vampire dogs drop sheep hearts at this yellow dog's feet. He tossed the heart up like it was a ball, snapped it up."

The man smacked his lips. I could hear it over the phone. "I've got a place for him, if you catch him as well."

"If you pay us, we'll get him. There are no bonus dogs."

"Check with your husband on that."

I thought of the slimy black hole he'd dug.

"They say that if you take a piece of him, good things will come your way. People don't like to talk about him. He's taboo."

"They just don't want anyone else taking a piece of him."

We moved to a new hotel set amongst the rainforest. The walls were dark green in patches, the smell of mould strong, but it was pretty with birdsong and close to the waterfalls which meant we could make an early start.

We ate in their open air restaurant; fried fish, more coconut milk, Greek meatballs. Gina didn't like mosquito repellant, thinking it clogged her pores with chemicals, so she was eaten alive by them.

"Have you called Joe?" she asked me over banana custard.

"Have you?" We smiled at each other; wife and sister ignoring him, back home and alone.

"We should call him. Does he know what we're doing?"

"I told him, but you know how he is." She was a good sister, visiting him weekly, reading to him, taking him treats he chewed but didn't seem to enjoy.

We drank too much Fijian beer and we danced around the snooker table, using the cues as microphones. No one seemed bothered, least of all the waiters.

The next morning, we called a cab to drop us at the top of the waterfall. You couldn't drive down any further. In the car park, souvenir sellers sat listlessly, their day's takings a few coins that jangled in their pockets. Their faces marked with lines, boils on their shins, they leaned back and stared as we gathered our things together.

"I have shells," one boy said.

"No turtles," Gina said, flipping her head at him to show how disgusting that trade was to her.

"Not turtles. Beetles. The size of a turtle."

He held up the shell to her. There was a smell about it, almost like an office smell; cleaning fluids, correcting fluids, coffee brewed too long. The shell was metallic gray and marbled with black lines. Claws out the side, small, odd, clutching snipers. I had seen, had eaten, prawns with claws like this. Bluish and fleshy, I felt like I was eating a sea monster.

"From the third waterfall," the seller said. "All the other creatures moved up when the dogs moved into Nine Waterfall."

I'm in the right place, I thought. "So there are dogs in the waterfall?"

"Vampire dogs. They only come out for food. They live way down."

An older vendor hissed at him. “Don’t scare the nice ladies. They don’t believe in vampire dogs.”

“You’d be surprised what I believe in,” Gina said. She touched one finger to the man’s throat. “I believe that you have a secret not even your wife knows. If she learns of it, she will take your children away.”

“No.”

“Yes.” She gave the boy money for one of the shells and opened her large bag to place it inside.

He said, “You watch out for yellow dog. If you sacrifice a part of him you’ll never be hungry again. But if you fail you will die on the spot and no one will know you ever lived. If you take the right bit you will never be lonely again.”

I didn’t know that I wanted a companion for life.

As we walked, I said, “How did you know he had a secret?”

“All men have secrets.”

The first waterfall was overhung by flowering trees. It was a very popular picnic site. Although it took twenty minutes to reach, Indian women were there with huge pots and pans, cooking roti and warming dhal while the men and children swam. I trailed my hand in the water; very cool, not the pleasant body-temperature water of the islands, but a refreshing briskness.

Birdsong here was high and pretty. More birds than I’d seen elsewhere; broadbills, honey-eaters, crimson and masked parrots, and velvet doves. Safe here, perhaps. The ground was soft and writhing with worms. The children collected them for bait, although the fish were sparse. Down below, the children told us, were fish big enough to feed a family of ten for a week. They liked human bait, so men would dangle their toes in. I guessed they were teasing us about this.

The path to the second waterfall was well-trodden. The bridge had been built with good, treated timber and seemed sturdy.

The waterfall fell quietly here. It was a gentler place. Only the fisherman sat by the water's edge; children and women not welcome. The fish were so thick in the water they could barely move. The fishermen didn't bother with lines; they reached in and grabbed what they wanted.

Gina breathed heavily.

"Do you want to slow down a bit? I don't think we should dawdle, but we can slow down," I said.

"It's not that. It's the fish. I don't usually get anything from fish, but I guess there's so many of them. I'm finding it hard to breathe."

The men stood up to let us past.

"There are a lot of fish," I said. Sometimes the obvious is the only thing to say. "Where do they come from?" I asked one of the men. "There are so few up there." I pointed up to the first waterfall.

"They come from underground. The centre of the earth. They are already cooked when we catch them, from the heat inside."

He cut one open to demonstrate and it was true; inside was white, fluffy, warm flesh. He gestured it at me and I took a piece. Gina refused. The meat was delicate and sweet and I knew I would seek without finding it wherever else I went in the world.

"American?" the man said.

"New Zealand," Gina lied.

"Ah, Kiwi!" he said. "Sister!" They liked the New Zealanders better than Australians and Americans because of closer distance, and because they shared a migratory path. Gina could put on any accent; it was like she absorbed the vowel sounds.

I could have stayed at the second waterfall but we had a job to do, and Gina found the place claustrophobic.

"It's only going to get worse," I said. "The trees will close in on us and the sky will vanish."

She grunted. Sometimes, I think, she found me very stupid and shallow. She liked me better than almost anybody else did, but sometimes even she rolled her eyes at me.

The third waterfall was small. There was a thick buzz of insects over it. I hoped not mosquitoes; I'd had dengue fever once before and did not want haemorrhagic fever. I stopped to slather repellant on, strong stuff which repelled people as well.

The ground was covered with small, green shelled cockroaches. They were not bothered by us and I could ignore them. The ones on the tree trunks bothered me more. At first I thought they were bark, but then one moved. It was as big as my head and I couldn't tell how many legs. It had a jaw which seemed to click and a tail like a scorpion which it kept coiled.

"I wouldn't touch one," Gina said.

"Really? Is that a vision you had?"

"No. they just look nasty," she said, and we shared a small laugh. We often shared moments like that, even at Joe's bedside.

Gina stumbled on a tree root the size of a man's thigh.

"You need to keep your eyes down," I said. "Downcast. Modest. Can you do that?"

"Can you?"

"Not really."

"Joe always liked 'em feisty."

Gina's breath came heavy now and her cheeks reddened.

"It's going to be tough walking back up."

"It always is. I don't even know why you're dragging me along. You could manage this alone."

"You know I need you to gauge the mood. That's why."

"Still. I'd rather not be here."

"I'll pay you well. You know that."

"It's not the money, Rosie. It's what we're doing. Every time I come out with you it feels like we're going against nature. Like we're siding with the wrong people."

"You didn't meet the client. He's a nice guy. Wants to save his kid."

"Of course he does, Rosie. You keep telling yourself that."

I didn't like that; I've been able to read people since I was twelve and it became necessary. Gina's sarcasm always confused me, though.

At the fourth waterfall, we found huge, stinking mushrooms, which seemed to turn to face us.

Vines hung from the trees, thick enough we had to push them aside to walk through. They were covered with a sticky substance. I'd seen this stuff before, used as rope, to tie bundles. You needed a bush knife to cut it. I'd realized within a day of being here you should never be without a bush knife and I'd bought one at the local shop. I cut a dozen vines, then coiled them around my waist.

Gina nodded. "Very practical." She was over her moment, which was good. Hard to work as a team with someone who didn't want to be there.

What did we see at the fifth waterfall? The path here was very narrow. We had to walk one foot in front of the other, fashion models showing off.

There were no vines here. The water was taken by one huge fish, the size of a Shetland pony. The surface of the water was covered with roe and I wondered where the mate was. Another underground channel? It would have to be a big one. It would be big but confining. My husband is confined in a similar fashion. I'm happy with him that way. He can't interfere with my business. Tell me how to do things.

At the sixth waterfall, we saw our first dog. It was very small and had no legs. Born that way? It lay in the pathway unmoving, and when I nudged it, I realised it was dead.

Gina clutched my arm. Her icy fingers hurt and I could feel the cold through my layers of clothing.

"Graveyard," she said. This is their graveyard.""

The surface of the sixth pool was thick with belly-up fish. At the base of the trees, dead insects like autumn leaves raked into a pile.

And one dead dog. I wondered why there weren't more.

"He has passed through the veil," Gina said, as if she were saying a prayer. "We should bury him."

"We could take him home to the client. He already has a hole dug in his backyard. He's kind of excited at the idea of keeping dogs there."

Is there a name for a person who takes pleasure in the confinement of others?

We reached the seventh waterfall.

We heard yapping, and I stiffened. I opened my bag and put my hand on a dog collar, ready. Gina stopped, closed her eyes.

"Puppies," she said. "Hungry."

"What sort?"

Gina shook her head. We walked on, through a dense short tunnel of wet leaves.

At the edge of the seventh waterfall there was a cluster of small brown dogs. Their tongues lapped the water (small fish, I thought) and when we approached, the dogs lifted their heads, widened their eyes and stared.

"Gaze Dogs," I said.

These were Gaze Dogs like I'd never seen before. Huge eyes. Reminded me of the spaniel with the brain too big.

"Let's rest here, let them get used to us," Gina said.

I glanced at my watch. We were making good time; assuming we caught a vampire dog with little trouble, we could easily make it back up by the sunfall.

"Five minutes."

We leaned against a moss-covered rock. Very soft, damp, with a smell of underground.

The Gaze Dogs came over and sniffled at us. One of the puppies had deep red furrows on its back; dragging teethmarks. I had seen this sort of thing after dog fights, dog attacks. Another had a deep dent in its side, filled with dark red scab and small yellow pustules. Close up, we could see most of the dogs were damaged in some way.

"Food supply?" Gina said.

I shuddered. Not much worried me, but these dogs were awful to look at.

One very small dog nuzzled my shoe, whimpering. I picked it up; it was light, weak. I tucked it into my jacket front. Gina smiled at me. "You're not so tough!"

"Study purposes." I put four more in there; they snuggled up and went to sleep.

She seemed blurry to me; it was darker than before. Surely the sun wasn't further away. We hadn't walked that far. My legs ached as if I had been hiking for days.

At the eighth waterfall we found the vampire dogs. Big, gazing eyes, unblinking, watching every move we made. The dogs looked hungry, ribs showing, stomachs concaved.

"They move fast," Gina whispered, her eyes closed. "They move like the waterfall."

The dogs swarmed forward and knocked me down. Had their teeth into me in a second, maybe two.

The feeling of them on me, their cold, wet paws heavy into my flesh, but the heat of them, the fiery touch of their skin, their sharp teeth, was so shocking I couldn't think for a moment; then I pulled a puppy from my jacket and threw it.

Their teeth already at work, the dogs saw the brown flash and followed it.

They moved so fast I could still see fur when they were gone.

I threw another puppy and another vampire dog peeled off with a howl. The first puppy was almost drained, its body flatter, as if the vampires sucked out muscle, too.

"Quick," Gina said. "Quick." She had tears in her eyes, feeling the pain of the puppies, their deaths, in her veins.

I threw a third puppy and we ran down, away from them. We should have run up, but they filled the path that way.

I scrabbled in my bag, pulling out the things I'd need to drop three of them. Or four.

We heard a huffing noise; an old man coughing up a lifetime. We were close to the base and the air was so hard to breathe we both panted. Gina looked at me.

"It must be the alpha. The yellow dog."

It seemed to me she stopped breathing for a moment.

"We could try to take a piece of him. We'd never be lonely again, if we did that."

The vampire dogs growled at us, wanting more puppies. The last two were right against my belly; I couldn't reach them easily and I didn't want to.

"I don't want to see the ninth waterfall," Gina said. I shook my head. If the Vampire dogs were this powerful, how strong would their alpha be?

"I'll take three of them down quietly; the others won't even notice. Then we'll have to kick our way out."

She nodded.

We turned around and he was waiting. That dog.

He was crippled and pitiful but still powerful. His tail, his ears and his toes had been cut off by somebody brave. Chunks of flesh were gone from his side. People using him as sacrifice for gain.

Gina was impressive; I could see she was in pain. Was she feeling the yellow dog's pain? She was quiet with it, small grunts. She walked towards him.

The closer she got to the dog the worse it seemed to get. "I want to lay hands on him, give him comfort," Gina said.

The dog was the ugliest I've ever seen. Of all the strays who've crossed my path here, this one was the most aggressive. This dog would make a frightening man, I thought. A man I couldn't control. Drool streamed down his chin.

He sat slouched, rolled against his lower back. Even sitting he reached to my waist.

All four legs were sprawled. He reminded me of an almost-drunk young man, wanting a woman for the night and willing to forgo that last drink, those last ten drinks, to achieve one. Sprawled against the bar, legs wide, making the kind of display men can.

His fur was the colour of piss, that golden colour you don't want to look at too hard, and splotched with mud, grease, and something darker.

One ear was half bitten off. The other seemed to stand straight up, unmoving, like a badly-made wooden prosthetic.

One lip was split, I think; it seemed blurry at this distance.

He licked his balls. And his dog's lipstick stuck out, fully twelve centimetres long, pink and waving.

Thousands of unwanted puppies in there.

He wasn't threatening; I felt sorry for him. He was like a big boy with the reputation of being a bully, who has never hurt anyone.

But when we got close to the yellow dog I realized he was perfect, no bits missing. An illusion to seduce us to come closer. Gina stepped right up to him.

"Gina! Come back!" but she wouldn't.

"If I comfort him, he will send me a companion. A lifetime companion," she said.

"Come live with me!" I said. "We'll take some gaze dogs, rescue them. We'll live okay."

He reared back on his hind legs and his huge skull seemed to reach the trees. He lifted his great paw high.

Around our feet, the vampire dogs swarmed. I grabbed one. Another. I sedated them and shoved them in my carry bag.

The Yellow dog pinned Gina with his paws. The vampire dogs surrounded him, a thick blue snarling band around him.

I threw my last two gaze dogs at them but they snapped at them too quickly. I had no gun. I picked up three rocks and threw one, hard. Pretended it was a baseball and it was three balls, two strikes.

The vampire dogs swatted the rock away as if it were a dandelion. I threw another, and the last, stepping closer each time.

The yellow dog had his teeth at Gina's throat and I ran forward, thinking only to tear her away, at least drag her away from his teeth.

The vampire dogs, though, all over me, biting my eyes, my ears, my lips.

I managed to throw them off, though perhaps they let me.

The yellow dog sat crouched, his mouth covered with blood. At his paws, I thought I saw hair, but I wondered: what human has been down here? Who else but me would come this far?

I backed away. Two sleeping vampire dogs in my bag made no noise and emitted no odour; I was getting away with it. They watched me go, their tongues pink and wet. The yellow dog; again, from afar he looked kindly. A dear old faithful dog. I took two more vampire dogs down, simple knock out stuff in a needle, and I put them in my bag. A soft blanket waited there; no need to damage the goods.

I picked up another gaze dog as I walked. This one had a gouge in his back, but his fur was pale brown, the colour of milk chocolate. He licked me. I put him down my jacket, then picked up another for a companion.

It took me hours to reach the top. Time did not seem to pass, though. Unless I'd lost a whole day. When I reached second waterfall, there were the same fishermen. And the families at first waterfall, swimming, cooking and eating as if there was no horror below them. They all waved at me but none offered food or drink.

The souvenir salesmen were there at the top. "Shells?" they said. "Buy a shell. No sale for a week, you know. No sale. You will be the first." I didn't want a shell; they came from the insects I'd seen below and didn't want to be reminded of them.

I called a cabbie to take me to my hotel. I spent another day, finalizing arrangements for getting the dogs home (you just need to know who to call) then I checked out of my room.

The Doctor was happier than I'd thought he'd be. Only two dogs had survived, but they were fit and healthy and happily sucked the blood out of the live chicken he provided them.

"You were right; you work well alone," he said. "You should dump that husband of yours. You can manage alone."

I'd just come from visiting Joe and his dry-eyed gaze, his flaccid fingers, seemed deader than ever. The nurses praised me up, glad there was somebody for him. "Oh, you're so good," they said. "So patient and loyal. He has no one else." Neither do I, I told them.

A month or so later, the Doctor called me. He wanted to show me the dogs; prove he was looking after them properly.

A young woman dressed in crisp, white clothes answered the door.

"Come in!" she said.

"You know who I am?"

Leading me through the house, she gave me a small wink. "Of course."

I wasn't sure I liked that.

She led me outside to the backyard; it was different. He'd tiled the hole and it was now a fish pond. The yard was neater, and lounge chairs and what looked like a bar were placed in a circle. Six people sat in the armchairs, reading magazines, sipping long drinks.

"He didn't tell me there was a party."

"Take a seat. Doctor will be with you shortly," the young woman said. Three of the guests looked at their watches as if waiting for an appointment.

I studied them. They were not a well group. Quiet and pale, all of them spoke slowly and lifted their glasses gently as if in pain or lacking strength. They all had good, expensive shoes. Gold jewellery worn with ease. The Doctor had some wealthy friends.

They made me want to leap up, jump around, show off my health.

The young woman came back and called a name. An elderly woman stood up.

"Thank you, nurse," she said. It all clicked in then; I'd been right. The Doctor was charging these people for treatment.

It was an hour before he dealt with his patients and called me in.

The vampire dogs rested on soft blankets. They were bloated, their eyes rolling. They could barely lift their heads. Bleeding therapy was back with a profit, even if leeches were out.

"You see my dogs are doing well."

"And so are you, I take it. How's your son?"

Doctor laughed. "You know there's no son."

He gave me another drink. His head didn't bobble. We drank vodka together, watching the vampire dogs prowl his yard, and a therapist would say my self-loathing led me to sleep with him.

I crawled out of the client's bed at two or three am, home to my Gaze Dogs. They were healing well and liked to chew my couch. They jumped up at me, licking and yapping, and the three of us sat on the floor, waiting for the next call to come in.

The Gate Theory

Jesus fuck, the road is long. You don't think about distance in Canberra, where a drive to Sydney takes three hours, to Melbourne seven, but then there are towns along the way.

Civilisation.

Out here there is nothing but the long, red road.

My sister Lillian comes and goes. She's only vaguely interested in Jake, the guy driving; wait till later, when I have at him. Then she'll spark up. Now, she doesn't realise he's actually pretty attractive underneath those dusty clothes.

And he's quiet, which is good.

He met me in Katherine, straight off the Darwin bus, greeting me like an old friend. I wasn't sure yet where he stood on the community itself. I was there to shut it down, "in a peaceful and quiet manner," I'd been told. "No fuss." This was the project that would set me ahead, put me high up on the 'must promote' list. I wanted to get it right.

Would he try to convince me otherwise? I didn't mind him trying but it wouldn't get him anywhere.

Lillian whispered, "Do we like him?" and I laughed, then coughed to cover it up.

I wondered if he could smell her and thought it was me, so I pulled out some ylang ylang hand cream to mask it.

My sister Lilian has a smell about her now. Roses gone brown on the edges, or a glass of wine left out overnight. It gets stronger when she thinks I'm heading for trouble. She's addicted to trouble. She always was an addict although it looked like I was. She loved my failures, fed off them like a hungry man sucks up spaghetti.

Every time she found me asleep in the gutter, every time she washed my face, every time she scared off another shit boyfriend; that's the stuff that made her feel good.

We were always better when there was a third. Someone we could both focus on. Otherwise it was like two relentless beams of light directed at each other.

If she had a boyfriend, or I did, we'd freak them out with our intensity. If we both had one at the same time it was okay but that somehow rarely happened.

When we were kids it was the same with best friends. We'd become obsessed with them, buying them presents, making them things, always wanting to be with them until they tired of us and walked away.

Addictive personalities, even then.

Growing up I always knew how much better she was. She got the good marks at school; she had all the future.

After she died things changed for me. Did she have to die for that to happen? That's what my biographer will ask.

I changed. I was lucky enough not to have a record, and my parents put me through Uni as a mature-age student, in some ways pretending Lillian never existed, that I had always been the good daughter, not her. That I was 18 and nothing bad ever happened.

I took a large sip of water.

"So you work in Canberra?" Jake asked. "That must suck."

"I like it, actually. Get to be in the heart of things. In the middle of reality."

He snorted at that. "Not much reality down there. Man-made lakes, pollies, fake people."

I crossed my legs so my skirt hitched mid-thigh. Faced my knees towards him. "The only thing I've ever had to fake is an orgasm. And that wasn't my fault."

He laughed and looked sidelong.

"Eyes on the road," I said. "Don't want to kill anyone."

Lillian snuck her hand into mine. She doesn't like it when I talk about death.

The sex stuff? She loves that.

I don't recommend holding your sister's hand while she dies. It's like opening up a gate, like an electrical gate is opened by the touching of the hand and the ghost gets through.

It's true. Every ghost that hangs around is here because some idiot held their hand and opened the gate.

This is my gate theory.

I watched her life shut down. She seemed to blur, and I thought it was because I was crying and my eyesight wasn't sharp, but then it came into focus and she seemed to hover above herself until she disappeared.

It was hard to get warm after that. Even on a sunny day I felt chilled, as if someone stood over me, blocking the light. I ignored it; pretended she wasn't there for a long time.

Until.

Until I met Giles. The first man who was sadder than me, had a worse life, who hated himself more. Our seduction was comparing awful behaviour, "I drowned my own dog," was his, and he said, "And I think I'm a father but I'm not sure and don't care, and I drink a bottle of vodka a night and have no family to speak of and no friends."

I told him about Lillian, how she'd be alive today if it wasn't for me, a great artist or actress or some kind of famous thing. I said I didn't mean for it to happen and yet it had.

And then we made love. He hadn't done it before, not properly.

"I don't deserve this," he kept saying.

"No, you don't," I said, but I didn't deserve happiness either.

He stopped partway through, looked over his shoulder. "How did you manage that? Lick my feet when your mouth is way up here?"

But it was her, my sister, squatting naked on the end of my bed, her tongue lolled out, her flaps swollen and red like tongues as well, all glistening.

Later, he curled into a ball as if I'd beaten him.

"Sad man," Lillian whispered. She was with me, now, and I heard her. "Sad, sad, sad man."

She's sitting in the back seat, legs spread. She won't stop fiddling with herself.

"We can have a break here if you like. Well, we better."

It was a small hotel. Flies everywhere. Men on the verandah, leaning over it, staring.

"I can drive for a while," I said.

"Sure. I still need to…"

He wasn't sure if he was supposed to be formal with me. Court shoes, neat skirt, silk blouse. Hair in bun. I looked official.

"This the Government lady?" one of them asked. "Gonna shut the abos down?"

Jake nodded.

"Only trouble is they come into Durram Downs," another man said. "Become our problem, don't they? All right for you, getting them off your backs."

"Beer?" Jake said.

My sister nodded. Floating around the men, sniffing at them. She loves a worker. Loves the rough trade.

"I really don't want a beer. Maybe when we get there."

"Just leave the bastards be," one man said. "They'll be dead before long and no one will have to worry about them."

I wasn't going to argue with an idiot.

We didn't speak much. I concentrated on the road. On keeping to a reasonable speed (although Jake told me no one gave a shit about the limit out here) and avoiding the animals that seemed to be using the highway like we did.

As we approached Durrum Downs I said, "Are they all going to have an opinion for me here?"

"'Fraid so. It affects all of us."

"So, what? You think we should leave them alone?"

"Some people think so."

"But they're killing themselves. It's not like they're happy and healthy."

I'd been sent here because there had been "a rash of deaths". A rash of suicides, as if the deaths were a nuisance, an itch, and all that's needed is the application of ointment and the skin will be smooth again.

There were two hotels in the town and I'd chosen the right one; it had an automatic door and air conditioning. The other one was at the end of town, near the small doctor's office. I hate the smell of anything medical.

Not your fault, people said, but everyone knew it was. I couldn't get myself to the clinic so Lillian showed up and took me, forcing me into the shower, making me wear her kind of clothes.

That's all I wear, these days. Am I stepping in for her? Living the life she should have led?

Maybe.

But it's better than the shit life I was living for myself.

Not your fault that whoever it was (they never did find out) was refused service at the clinic and came out wild, really wild. Banged into us both but I kept my footing. She didn't and into the path of the car.

I never let go her hand.

The hotel room was fine. Small, and decorated in nasty mustard colours, but it was clean, at least. The air conditioner didn't work but the fan did.

There are homeless people in Canberra but I rarely see them. They've got their spots; between pillars, in the alleyways, and I don't go there.

Here, though…

We walked out to find food, and we had to step over them. I tripped over one, who grunted, and then my eyes came into focus and I could see them all.

"So many people on the streets," I said as we entered the town's only restaurant. "Chinese and Australian," it was called.

"Them?" Jake said. "Yeah, well. They don't like living in houses."

I watched them through a split in the dirty curtains. Like ghosts; most people looked through them.

We drank beer because it was so hot and the wine list was Red or White. I drank a lot. Thirsty. When I burped, and he laughed, not at me, but affectionately, I knew I'd sleep with him.

I'd probably known from the moment I saw him, actually.

Known that I'd do it, but that laugh confirmed that he would.

At the hotel, I did the fumble with the key thing. It wasn't fake; my sister was so excited she grabbed at my fingers, wanting to hurry me up, and it didn't help.

We had a six pack of beer and I had a balcony, so we sat out there, slapping insects, sharing stories. He went into the bathroom. My sister followed him. I heard a shout, so he'd seen her.

"Jeez. It feels as if there's a hole in the wall and someone's staring in," he said.

He shuddered.

"We better turn the lights off, then," I said, and I led him inside.

Jake proved to be slightly more interesting than I thought he would. Bigger dick, for one thing. And while he professed to a warm heart, he didn't mind a bit of pain.

The ceiling fan provided little relief. It was too hot with two of us in the bed, so he went to his room, kissing me quite lovingly.

"We'll head out early," he said. "Before it gets really hot."

A short drive the next morning. I'd ducked out first thing and bought him a small gift; just a beer glass, but I thought it was a nice gesture. He looked a bit stunned. He'd get used to it. I tended to give my people lots of gifts.

"Just warning you, the place is a shit hole."

"That's why we're shutting it down," I said. "Makes sense."

"Only problem is they all end up in town where no one wants them."

"Programs will be set up. Extra teachers. That kind of thing. Much better for them."

He didn't answer. Was he thinking of all of those people on the streets? I'd heard a child crying in the night, but sometimes Lillian cried like that so it didn't bother me.

I had less sympathy than other people because yeah, it's hard to get out of the gutter but it's not impossible.

I did it.

He pulled up at what was once the police station. The cops were the last to go.

The silence was enormous. No wind, no movement. The most incredible stillness. I felt set in resin, or made of glass. I felt as if a single step would crack the whole place open.

"Where is everyone?"

"Only ten of them left. The rest have seen sense and headed out. When the grocery store shut, most of them got it."

We walked to a large house up on stilts. It was brightly painted and someone had once cared about the garden because it was laid out neatly with pebble paths and a bird bath.

"They all shifted in here when the shop owner moved out. He was the only one of them who had any money. Shoulda seen what he charged for a beer."

"Did you come out here often?"

"Nah. Helped transport a few of them. Helped move the merchandise."

"Drink it, you mean."

He smiled. "You can talk," he said, and he grabbed me there, on the street, and kissed me hard and deep. I heard my sister roar and if there had been some place not full of flies, I might have.

Later. Save it for later.

We walked up the stairs. The stillness hadn't changed but I could hear a low murmuring.

He put his hand up to knock but I pushed the door open. They didn't own this place, they were squatters. You don't knock on the door for the benefit of squatters.

It was dark inside the house, well-shuttered against the heat. The fans were still, power long since shut down. We passed through the small entrance and into the room where they all sat.

What struck me first was how tired they all looked. I'd seen that weariness; hospital staff in the drug zone, into their thirtieth hour of a shift. Pure exhaustion and hopelessness.

"G'day," Jake said. "This is Emma Macquarie. She's gonna talk to you about moving."

They all tucked themselves in, pulled away from me.

"You might want to shut up, mate. Not helping," I said, but I winked and showed him the tip of my tongue so he knew I still loved him.

"Who's boss here?"

An elderly woman stood up. She was as tired as the rest of them, but her shoulders were straight and she walked right up to me, standing a metre or two away, looking into my eyes.

"No bosses here," she said.

"This one knows the country, though," one of the men said, making a gesture as if pointing with his lips at the old woman.

"You've got good family. Good people. Anywhere you live will be home. We'll make sure you stay together."

Yeah, we'd try. But seriously? Looking at the disparate ages? It probably wouldn't happen. They'd get used to it.

"This is our place. Always has been. You take us from here you cut off our breathing." And she sucked in a couple of hard lungsful of air to demonstrate.

I didn't believe that bullshit.

"All the buildings will fall down and no one will fix them."

"We can fix them," one of the men said quietly. "We fix things fine."

"And we can live outside in that guy," the grandmother said. She pointed out of the window. A giant baobab tree stood there, its limbs reaching out ten metres or so, its trunk almost as wide. It gaped open, looking like a brown vagina. I whispered this to Jake.

"Seriously? Don't you think so?" and that actually shocked him.

We went out into the backyard. There were fewer flies there, but a lot of canvases sitting out in the dust. "Part of the art," one of the men said.

To humour them I stepped inside the tree.

It was beautifully cool, but claustrophobic. There was a young boy resting there, on bright blankets. No pillow.

"He's pretty sick," the grandmother said. "Hot as."

"Where's the doctor?" and I'd fallen into the trap because no doctor came out here.

"We need doctors," they said, but I said, this is why you need to move. You know? It's not a human right to have medical care no matter where you live.

Heat radiated off the boy and I didn't want to go near him.

"Hold his hand," Jake said. "Show some compassion. Pretend you care."

For that shit I would fuck him again, later. Fuck him up, leave him so filled with self-loathing he'd never go at me again.

But I held the kid's hand. It was dry. Gritty.

"He really does need a hospital," I said. "If you lived close to the city we could facilitate that." It seemed astonishing how much they didn't get it. "We can take him now, if you like. We can fit about five of you in. Get your stuff later."

I counted in my head, thinking two minutes more holding the kid's hand would be enough. But my sister climbed onto the bed and squatted over his chest, looking into his eyes.

"He's about to go," she said. "Hold on tight."

I dropped his hand. Gate Theory. But the fuckwit picked it up. My idiot companion.

That boy was the first ghost in town.

His mother lay beside him in that massive tree trunk, weeping. The grandmother stroked her hair, murmuring beautiful words I could not understand but wish I'd heard myself, at least once.

Jake said, "We should leave them for today. We'll come back for them tomorrow."

I drove myself the next morning, not wanting his influence. There was noise in the back; calling, and wailing, and shouts.

The boy's mother had fashioned a noose, which she tied around the baobab tree. Her son floated close by, nodding, squeezing himself, as if excited, as if anticipating her arrival in his world with great delight.

"He loves you," I said.

I looked at Lillian. Her mouth was a tiny 'ooh', waiting to see what I'd do. This was my choice. A first for me for in a long time. Choosing as me. Not as Lillian.

The grandmother said, "What are you doing? You should stop her. She won't listen to us. Get your police friends in."

One of the men laughed. "Yeah so she can die in a cell."

They agreed.

"I'm not going to do anything," I said. "Can you see him? Your boy?"

They all nodded.

"I can see my sister as well," and I told them about her, the comfort she gave me. How happy she was; how the world to her was always happy, and she was never hungry and felt no sadness.

"Would we stay here?" the grandmother asked. "Would we stay here, in this place?" She tapped her chest to mean the land.

"I'm not sure. My sister comes with me everywhere. But our place is here," and I tapped my heart, too. "We have no other place."

She nodded.

That sense of peace and quiet hung over all of us.

"I can leave you to it, or I can stay," I said, knowing I would need to hold the hand of the last of them, at least."

"Please. Stay." The grandma kissed me.

One by one they went, holding hands. My sister did her best to welcome them. No one can shift you now, she said. This is your place.

The last man left alive was packed, ready to go. As if he could take it with him.

"We're done. We're finished," he said. His face was wet with tears, and the backs of his hands, from wiping.

"You'll live forever."

"But no new ones. No growing family. It ends here." He wept.

Some people are never satisfied.

They all slipped out like boiled broad beans slip from their skins.

Jake arrived, with a cop in tow.

"We thought there might be trouble. There often is. But figured you'd call if you were really in trouble. Jeez, it's a ghost town. Where are they?"

"They all left. All squeezed in the back of a ute," I said. "Left everything behind. But it's crap, all of it, anyway. They reckoned they had a place to go."

"They never showed up at Durrum."

"They're sorting themselves. Give them a couple of weeks," I told him. "They don't want to come into town. They're going to find a place deep out there. Where none of us can touch them."

"I didn't take you for a kind one," he said. I think he was genuinely surprised. "What about the kid?"

"He recovered," I said, although Jake had seen all that I had seen.

The ghosts were all hidden around the place; in the rocks, the trees, flattened in the red dirt. The men didn't look at all; as far as they were concerned it was over. They didn't care about evidence, or bodies, or anything.

I wondered if my sister would stay behind, but no. Already she was playing with herself, ready for a night of fun with the two men.

I was tired of it all, though, and keen to get out of there.

Jake watched me pack my few things. I kept waiting for him to tell me not to go; the longer I waited with the silence, the angrier I got.

He'd try to sleep with ordinary women, try to wipe the memory of me away, but he never would. I knew that but he didn't know it yet.

He got someone else to drive me to Katherine. I left him a note; he'd read it and realise what he'd lost.

Thing was, it was good for all. I did the thing I was sent out to do, and I did it peacefully. Quietly.

And all those people who wanted nothing to do with the real world?

They got their wish, too.